WHAT HAPPENED ON THE NIGHT

SHE DIED?

The report said Julie had been holding the knife that killed her. Had she picked it up to attack someone, or to defend herself?

Try as he would, Thanet couldn't visualize the quiet Julie lying in wait for her husband with a carving knife. Nor, for that matter, could he see Holmes calmly taking the knife to night school with the intention of killing her when he got home. Yet if he were guilty, it couldn't have been any other way, there wouldn't have been time. In any case, it was Julie's prints that were on the knife. Was it possible that Holmes could have killed her, that when she was dead he had simply taken her hand and pressed it around the dagger, holding it in the right position to give the impression she had been gripping it herself? He must ask Doc Mallard. In any case, his original objection still held: he could see Holmes driven to stabbing in a fit of jealous rage, perhaps, but this way? It didn't feel right.

Then, too, there was the question of why Julie had been dressed to go out.

Bantam Books offers the finest in classic and modern British murder mysteries.
Ask your bookseller for the books you have missed.

Agatha Christie

Death on the Nile
A Holiday for Murder
The Mousetrap and Other Plays
The Mysterious Affair at Styles
Poirot Investigates
Postern of Fate
The Secret Adversary
The Seven Dials Mystery
Sleeping Murder

Dorothy Simpson

Last Seen Alive
The Night She Died
Puppet for a Corpse
Six Feet Under
Close Her Eyes
coming soon: Element of Doubt

Sheila Radley

The Chief Inspector's Daughter
Death in the Morning
Fate Worse Than Death
Who Saw Him Die?

Elizabeth George

A Great Deliverance
coming soon: A Payment in Blood

Colin Dexter

Last Bus to Woodstock
The Riddle of the Third Mile
The Silent World of Nicholas Quinn
Service of All the Dead
The Dead of Jericho
The Secret of Annexe 3
Last Seen Wearing

John Greenwood

The Mind of Mr. Mosley
The Missing Mr. Mosley
Mosley by Moonlight
Murder, Mr. Mosley
Mists Over Mosley
What, Me, Mr. Mosley?

Ruth Rendell

A Dark-Adapted Eye
  (writing as Barbara Vine)
A Fatal Inversion
  (writing as Barbara Vine)

Marian Babson

Death in Fashion
Reel Murder
Murder, Murder Little Star
Murder on a Mystery Tour
Murder Sails at Midnight

Christianna Brand

Suddenly at His Residence
Heads You Lose

Dorothy Cannell

The Widows Club
coming soon: Down the Garden Path

Michael Dibdin

Ratking

THE NIGHT SHE DIED

Dorothy Simpson

BANTAM BOOKS
TORONTO · NEW YORK · LONDON · SYDNEY · AUCKLAND

THE NIGHT SHE DIED

A Bantam Book / published by arrangement with
Charles Scribner's Sons

PRINTING HISTORY

Charles Scribner's edition published September 1981
Bantam edition / September 1985
2nd printing . . . March 1989

A Mystery Guild Selection

Copyright under the Berne Convention.

ISBN 0-553-27772-3

Published simultaneously in the United States and Canada

Bantam Books are published by Bantam Books, a division of Bantam
Doubleday Dell Publishing Group, Inc. Its trademark, consisting of the
words ''Bantam Books'' and the portrayal of a rooster, is Registered
in U.S. Patent and Trademark Office and in other countries. Marca
Registrada. Bantam Books, 666 Fifth Avenue, New York, New York 10103.

PRINTED IN THE UNITED STATES OF AMERICA

O   11 10 9 8 7 6 5 4 3 2

For
KEITH

1

It was half past nine in the evening and Detective Inspector Luke Thanet was stretched out on the living-room carpet, staring at the ceiling. Despite the padding, the rolling-pin in the small of his back seemed to be cutting his spine in two. He cast an agonised glance at the clock. Only a minute had gone by since the last time he had looked. It seemed impossible that time could pass so slowly.

He heard Joan come downstairs and a moment later she put her head around the door. "I think he's gone off at last," she said. Ben, their one-year-old son, was teething. "At least he didn't wake Bridget. I'll make some coffee. How much longer?"

Another glance at the clock. "Ten minutes."

She grimaced in sympathy. "I shan't be long." She went out and he could hear her moving about in the kitchen next door.

Coffee, he told himself. Concentrate on coffee, concentrate on anything but the discomfort.

Two weeks ago, injudiciously heaving the lawn-mower out of the boot of his car, Thanet had joined the nation's army of back sufferers. His first reaction had been one of outrage. Why should this happen to him? Since then he had run the gamut of emotions, from anger with himself through frustration to despair. He had also suffered being massaged, pulled about, exercised and lectured by an astonishingly diminutive physiotherapist. How could someone so tiny have so much power in her hands, he had asked himself incredulously. And when, when was his back going to get better? Never before had he realised the value of what he had until now taken so carelessly for granted— his health. And he swore that never again, if it were ever restored to him, would he fail to appreciate it to the full. Meanwhile, here he was, doing his daily fifteen minutes on the rack (the rolling-pin), an exercise designed to "restore flexibility to the spine."

Joan came in carrying a tray. "Coffee," she said. "Shall I pour it now?"

Thanet shook his head, wincing at the stab of pain induced by even that tiny movement. "In a minute," he said, between his teeth. Then, "Talk, darling, for God's sake talk. What have you been up to today?"

They had scarcely seen each other this evening. Joan had eaten long before he arrived home and had spent most of the time since then upstairs, trying to get Ben off to sleep.

She poured out a cup of coffee for herself, sank down on to the settee with a sigh of relief. "Nothing much, really." She kicked her shoes off, tucked her feet up beneath her, sipped at her coffee. "No, that's not true. I went to the last day of the Dacre Exhibition."

"At the College of Art?"

"Yes. It's a pity you missed it. It was terrific. Her paintings are absolutely unique, like nothing I've ever seen before. They . . ."

The telephone rang.

Joan uncoiled herself wearily. "I'll get it. I hope it's not for you." But it was. "Yes, he's here," Thanet heard her say.

"Tell them to hold on, I'm coming," he called out, shooting a triumphant glance at the clock. He was going to cheat it of two minutes. Impossible, though, to raise himself into a sitting position. With a groan he rolled over on to his stomach, tensing against the pain, raised himself slowly on to hands and knees and finally, moving very carefully, managed to stand up.

"Yes, yes," he said irritably into the telephone. "Of course I'm fit." He scowled at Joan who was raising her eyebrows in admonitory disbelief and turned his back on her. "All right," he said when he had replaced the receiver, "but what do you expect me to say? That I've got one foot in the grave?"

She followed him to the cloakroom, laid her hand affectionately against his cheek and stretched up to kiss him. "Don't wait up, love," he said. "I may be late."

Already, she could see, his mind was moving ahead, away from her. "Something serious?"

He shrugged into his coat, wincing, and nodded. "Murder, they seem to think. A young housewife."

Joan stepped back, relinquishing him. "Take care, then," she said.

It was too early for the pubs, cinemas and bingo-halls to have discharged their nightly crowds and the centre of the town was more or less deserted as Thanet headed for Gladstone Road. He found it without difficulty, a quiet cul-de-sac tucked away behind an area of densely packed terraced houses. As he turned into it his headlights briefly illuminated a stretch of rough grass and tangled trees on the other side of the road. This, he realised, must slope down to the railway line; as he drew up behind the other cars a train thundered by, invisible at the foot of the embankment.

As he eased himself out of his car he was glad to see that it was Detective Sergeant Mike Lineham who came forward to meet him. He enjoyed working with Lineham, who was both intelligent and thorough and would one day be a first-rate detective, if he could only overcome an irritating diffidence. His summing-up of the situation was typically concise.

"A young woman, sir. Name of Julie Holmes. Body found by her husband when he got home from night school—accompanied by a friend. She's been stabbed in the chest. A kitchen knife, by the look of it."

Becoming aware that Lineham's short, staccato sentences and air of urgency were having the effect of hurrying him along, Thanet deliberately stopped and stood still. Lineham, taken unawares, found himself at the gate of the house alone. He turned, unconsciously subsiding into an attitude of resignation. He ought to have known better by now, he told himself as he watched Thanet's head turn slowly, questingly, from left to right.

Whereas many detectives would hurry straight to the side of the body, Thanet always liked to feel his way into a case. "It's worth taking time to absorb first impressions properly," he'd told Lineham once, when they were working on the first murder they'd ever tackled together. "If I don't, they lose their impact. Time and again I've regretted rushing into things. Now I never do. A few minutes' delay at the start of a case will rarely hold things up and might save hours of work later on."

Now, Thanet gazed about him at Gladstone Road. The place in which someone chooses to live can reveal a great deal about him, he believed, and this place was . . . he groped for the word . . . secretive, yes, that was it. Gladstone Road definitely had a secretive air about it. It was about two hundred yards long. Most of it, right from the corner where one turned into it up to the boundary of the Holmes's garden, was taken up by some sort of yard, a builder's yard by the look of it, silent and deserted now. Thanet took a few steps back along the road to peer at the black and white sign high up on the close-boarded fence which surrounded it, the street lamp in front of the Holmes's house throwing just enough light to make it legible. *R. Dodson and Sons, Builders*, he read.

It looked as though at some point (the nineteen-thirties, probably, by the look of the Holmes's house) Dobson had decided to sacrifice part of his yard in order to make some ready cash, for the remainder of the short street had been divided up into two plots of equal size. Something however—the war?—had prevented him from building the second house; beyond the Holmes house and separated from it by a similar high close-boarded fence was a patch of waste ground. Why, Thanet wondered, had it not been built upon since? Lack of funds, perhaps, followed by the dawning realisation that here was an appreciating asset?

Beyond the empty plot, closing off the end of the cul-de-sac, was a wire-mesh fence. Set into it, over to the right where the ground started to slope down for the railway embankment was what looked like a metal swing-gate. Beyond the fence stood a coppice of trees, their restless branches creating a shifting, irregular silhouette of denser darkness against the night sky.

Yes, Thanet thought, anyone choosing to live in Gladstone Road would value privacy above all. He took one last, comprehensive look around, gave an approving pat to the lamppost beside him, then transferred his attention to Lineham who was shifting as unobtrusively as possible from one foot to another in an attempt to hide his impatience. "Right," he said, "let's go inside."

Lineham led the way with the alacrity of a retriever anxious to show his master a particularly juicy bone. Thanet followed more slowly, studying the house as he went. As he had already noted, it was of typical nineteen-thirties construction, with a front door to one side set back in a shallow, open porch, and bay windows on both floors.

"Round the back, sir. The body's just inside the front door."

Thanet followed without comment.

Lineham led the way through a small, square kitchen furnished with a formica table and two matching, metal-legged chairs into a narrow hall where a photographer and two fingerprint men were already at work. Thanet nodded approvingly at Lineham, pleased to see that the sergeant had trusted his own judgement sufficiently to get things moving without waiting for Thanet's arrival. Seeing Thanet, the men retreated a few steps up the staircase to allow him access to the body.

And there she was.

Thanet always hated this moment. No matter how

often he experienced it, no matter who the victim was, he could never quench this initial pang of pity, of regret for a life cut short. Almost at once he was able to become detached again, aware that emotional involvement could cripple his judgement, but this moment could never leave him unmoved and he was not sure that he would want it to. As he lowered himself gingerly to kneel beside the body, however, his face remained impassive. Many of his colleagues, he knew, would regard such feelings as weakness.

Julie Holmes had been young, not more than twenty-five, Thanet guessed. She lay sprawled on her back, her long hair a pool of spun gold on the uncarpeted floorboards, arms outflung and legs askew. She had, Thanet thought sadly, been a very pretty girl, perhaps even a beautiful one. Difficult to judge how animation would have affected that delicately modelled face, those deep-blue eyes. He glanced up at the photographer. "Have you finished with her?"

"Yes, sir."

Thanet closed her eyes. Let the others think what they would. Then he swiftly finished his examination. The girl was wearing a coat of brown herringbone tweed and had been stabbed right through it; the handle of the knife still protruded from her chest. There appeared to have been very little bleeding, but it was difficult to tell; the clothes she was wearing beneath the coat might well have absorbed a great deal. Pinned to the left lapel of the coat was a striking piece of jewellery, an enamelled brooch some three inches long in the design of a mermaid. Waist-length golden hair flowed modestly over the upper half of the mermaid's body, above the iridescent blue scales of the tail. Thanet could not decide whether he liked it or not. Mermaids had curious associations, an aura of paradoxically sexless nakedness... He glanced around. "Handbag?"

Lineham shook his head. "No sign of it. I've had a quick look."

Thanet struggled to his feet, wryly aware of the self-restraint Lineham was exercising in refraining from extending a hand to help. Thanet's touchiness on the subject of his back was well known. "Where's the husband?"

"In there," Lineham indicated the closed door beside them, "with the friend who was present when he found the body. And Constable Bingham."

"Right. Doc Mallard been yet? No? Well, let me know when he gets here. I'm going to have a word with Holmes. How many men have we got here?" Swiftly Thanet organised a search of the premises, the house-to-house enquiries, and then went into the living-room.

It was a room of curious contrasts. Like the hall, it was uncarpeted and there were no curtains at the windows. There was, however, a luxurious three-piece suite upholstered in gold and some expensive hi-fi equipment as well as a colour television set. In the bay window a gleaming sewing-machine stood on a long table on which were heaped swathes of cream and gold brocade.

The uniformed constable who had been standing just inside the door received Thanet's unspoken message and slipped out. Thanet turned his attention to the other two occupants of the room, only one of whom had looked up when he entered. This was a clearly angry young man in duffel coat and jeans who was standing in front of the empty fireplace, legs apart and hands thrust deep into his coat pockets. He was scowling at Thanet through a profusion of ginger hair. "Look here," he burst out, taking a step forward.

"Just one moment, sir," Thanet said, turning to the other man, who was sitting on the edge of one of the armchairs, leaning forward, head in hands. "Mr Holmes?"

The man slowly lifted a dazed face.

"Detective Inspector Thanet, Sturrenden CID. I'm sorry to have to impose myself on you at a time like this. . . ."

"I should bloody well think so! I—" cut in Holmes's friend.

"Just a moment, sir, please. But there are some

questions I really must ask," Thanet went on, turning back to Holmes.

"Questions! Where d'you think that'll get you? Why don't you leave this poor devil alone and—"

Thanet held up his hand. "Look Mr . . . ?"

"Byfleet. And I—"

"It's all right, Des," Holmes said unexpectedly. He passed his hand wearily over eyes and forehead. "I don't mind. The police have to do their job. Go on, Inspector."

"But he's told it all once," persisted Byfleet. "Does he have to go through it all over again?"

"It's all right, Des," Holmes repeated. "It's got to be done."

His accent was definitely not Kentish, Thanet thought. A Londoner? He sat down opposite Holmes and said gently, "If you could tell me exactly what happened this evening then, sir, right from the time you got home from work."

Holmes, it seemed, was the manager of the local branch of Homeright Supermarkets. He had arrived home from work this evening at about twenty past six, as usual. His wife was there before him—she, too, worked locally, in the office of an estate agent—and they had supper together before Holmes left for his evening class at a quarter to seven. She had said that she was going to spend the evening working on the living-room curtains.

Holmes and Byfleet (who lived in a neighbouring village and had been on his way to the station) had walked back from the Technical College together, arriving in Gladstone Road at about twenty past nine. Byfleet had parted from Holmes at the gate but a few moments later had been called back by a frantic shout from Holmes, who had found Julie's body sprawled just inside the front door. They had telephoned the police and an ambulance at once, but it was obvious that she was already dead.

"Your wife was wearing a coat," Thanet said. "You're sure she said nothing about going out?"

"No. I told you, she said she was going to work on the curtains." He nodded at the mounds of material on the long table.

"Have you any idea where she might have gone? To visit a friend, perhaps?"

Holmes shook his head. "She didn't have any friends here yet. We only moved in six weeks ago. The only people she knew were the ones at work, and none of them live anywhere near."

Holmes had apparently been offered a transfer to the Sturrenden branch of Homeright in October, six months ago. At that time he and his wife had been living in Brixton. They had at once started house-hunting, coming down to Sturrenden each weekend, but it had proved impossible to find the sort of house they wanted at a price they could afford. When the time came for Holmes to take up the appointment in early December he had had to go into lodgings, his wife staying on in London. Shortly afterwards they had found the house in Gladstone Road and had moved in as soon as completion took place, some twelve weeks later.

Thanet listened thoughtfully. So Holmes and his wife had been living apart for three months, long enough for either of them to have formed another attachment.

He transferred his attention to the belligerent Byfleet. "Mr Byfleet, I wonder if you could tell me exactly what you remember of arriving here this evening? I take it you and Mr Holmes attend the same evening class?"

Byfleet scowled. "Yes. And we was sitting next to each other all evening, if that's what you're getting at."

"And you agree with Mr Holmes about the time of your arrival here?"

"Yeah. I'm sure, because I was keeping my eye on the time, because of my train at nine-thirty. It takes six minutes to get to the station from here, along the footpath. Bang on twenty past nine it was, when we got here."

"The footpath?"

"The one at the end of the road. Cuts through that little wood, comes out near the station. Otherwise you have to go right round and over the bridge."

Thanet made a mental note to check the topography of the place thoroughly. "And you parted at the front gate?"

"Yeah. I'd gone, oh, fifteen, perhaps twenty yards along the road when John calls me back. Well, I ran. I mean, I could see straight away something was wrong. And there she was." Byfleet stopped, glanced uneasily at Holmes.

"You didn't actually see Mr Holmes go into the house?"

"No."

"The door wasn't locked," Holmes said suddenly. "I remember now, it was slightly ajar."

"You didn't mention this before," Thanet said sharply. "You're sure?"

"I'm sure, all right," Holmes said grimly. "I . . . I'd just forgotten. It . . . the whole thing was . . ."

Thanet waited, but Holmes did not go on.

"You didn't notice that the door was open, as you passed the house?" Thanet asked Byfleet.

"No. Why should I? We'd said good-bye, that was it, as far as I was concerned. I was thinking of my train."

"You didn't glance back at all?" Thanet persisted.

"No. No bloody no. Like I said, why should I?"

He would have to leave it for the moment, important though the point was. Thanet sighed. "All right, Mr Byfleet. So you could say that no more than fifteen or twenty seconds elapsed between the time you parted and the moment when you heard Mr Holmes shout?"

"Got it in one," said Byfleet sarcastically, folding his arms.

Time enough for Holmes to have stabbed his wife? Thanet thought. Time enough for her to have died? He glanced at Holmes who, eyes glazed, hands lying limply along the arms of the chair, seemed to have withdrawn himself from the proceedings. Thanet lowered his voice as he said to Byfleet, "Was there any sign of life when you first saw her?"

Byfleet shot a quick, concerned glance at Holmes and, apparently reassured that his friend had not heard the question, shook his head. "No." He looked at Holmes again and then, as if making up his mind, came to sit beside Thanet on the settee. When he next spoke the belligerence had gone and he said quietly, "Look, Inspector, John had nothing to do with it, honest he didn't. I was with him all evening, like I said and when we got here there just wouldn't have been time for him to . . . She was dead before ever he opened the door, I'd swear to that."

"Did either of you touch her?"

"No. John just stood there, like he'd been turned to stone. Well, I mean, you could tell just by looking at her with that bloody great knife sticking out of her."

He would have to ask Doc Mallard exactly how long it would have taken Julie Holmes to die, Thanet thought. As if the thought had conjured up the police surgeon there was a knock on the door. Lineham put his head around it. "Doc's here, sir."

"Right, I'm coming." Thanet stood up. "Thank you, Mr Byfleet. If you could bear with us just a little longer, I'll send someone in to take down your statement and then we'll get it typed out for you to sign tomorrow." At the door he paused. "Just one point, Mr Holmes." He waited, repeated the man's name twice before the dazed face turned towards him. "Mr Holmes," he said gently, "did your wife usually carry a handbag?"

A moment's pause and then, "Yes."

"What was it like?"

Holmes's forehead creased as he tried to focus his mind on the question. "Brown," he said at least. "Big. A shoulder thing."

Fairly obtrusive, by the sound of it. And certainly nowhere in this room, Thanet thought, glancing about him again. They'd check properly later on, of course, but . . . "Thank you," he said.

Constable Bingham moved unobtrusively back into the room as Thanet left.

In the narrow hall Mallard was bending over the body, his bald pate reflecting the light from the unshaded overhead bulb.

"I know, I know," he said testily, glancing up at Thanet. "Don't bother to say it. You can't imagine how boring it gets, hearing the same old questions every time."

Thanet and Lineham exchanged amused glances and waited in silence while Mallard continued his examination.

"Well," Mallard said, finally straightening up, "we won't know for sure, of course, until after the P.M., but it looks as though she died instantly. And," with a quelling glance as Thanet opened his mouth, "sticking my neck out as you always press me to do, I'd say, provisionally, that she's been dead between one and two hours. That, of course, is unofficial." He snapped his bag shut and stood up.

Thanet glanced at his watch. Half past ten. She must have died, if Mallard was right—and despite his caution he usually was—between eight-thirty and nine-thirty. No, between eight-thirty and nine-twenty, when her body had been found.

"Thanks Doc," he said.

Mallard scowled at him. He had never learned to receive compliments or expressions of gratitude gracefully. "How's that back of yours?"

"Improving."

"Hmph. Teach you to go doing damnfool things like heaving lawn-mowers about," growled Mallard, heading for the door.

"You can let them take her away now," Thanet said to Lineham. "And have another look around for her handbag—shoulder bag, actually. Brown, fairly big." He hurried after Mallard. Thanet was always punctilious in observing the courtesies. The police owed a great deal to the surgeons who frequently turned out of bed in the early hours to come to the scene of a murder and in any case, despite Mallard's testiness, Thanet was fond of him.

"How's young Ben?" Mallard asked as he tossed his case on to the passenger seat and settled himself behind the wheel.

"Teething," Thanet said tersely.

Mallard chuckled. "Ah, the joys of parenthood," he said. "And I'm told it gets worse, not better. Give my love to Joan—and watch that back, now." And with a smile and a wave, he was gone.

Thanet stood looking after him for a moment and then made his way thoughtfully back to the house, stepping back on to the lawn to avoid the ambulance men who were carrying a covered stretcher down the narrow front path. He watched as they slid their burden into the ambulance and closed the doors.

The end of a life, he thought. How inadequate were those few words to convey the aftermath of suffering always left by sudden death. And they marked, of course, only the beginning for him. Over the next days, weeks, months, perhaps, Julie Holmes would come alive for him in a unique way. Each of the people who had known her would have his own limited, individual view of her and Thanet would somehow have to reconcile all those views, assemble them into a composite whole.

It was possible, of course, that this might not happen, that the case might move to a swift conclusion. Most murders are committed by someone close to the victim and the most obvious person frequently turns out to be the murderer. Remembering that with good reason the police are always most suspicious of the person who finds the body, Thanet knew he must look long and hard at Holmes himself. Would there have been time for Holmes to have killed his wife, in the instant of opening the door? Impossible to say, as yet. Mallard's guess might be wrong. The girl might have been killed before her husband left for night school—analysis of her stomach contents would speak here. But if Mallard was right—as he usually was—and she had

been killed between eight-thirty and nine-twenty, why
had she been wearing her outdoor clothes? Had she
just come in, or had she been about to go out? Thanet
shook his head. There were too many imponderables as
yet. It was pointless to speculate at this stage.

Lineham met him at the front door, visibly excited.
"No sign of her handbag, sir. They'd finished fingerprinting
the kitchen, so I hope you don't mind, but I..."

"Don't be so apologetic, Mike," Thanet said testily.
"Of course you searched it, it's your job to use your
initiative, isn't it? It's the knife, I suppose?" And felt
ashamed of himself as Lineham visibly deflated. I really
must not let his diffidence irritate me, he told himself.
Apart from anything else it wasn't the best way to go
about building up the sergeant's confidence. "Come
on," he said, touching Lineham on the shoulder and
heading for the kitchen, "show me. It's an interesting
bit of news."

The kitchen knives were kept in a special board, in
one of the drawers. They had probably, Thanet thought,
been a wedding present. There should have been six,
but one, the carving knife by the look of it, was
missing. Looking at the largest knife of all, a gleaming
small butcher's cleaver, Thanet thought that they ought
to be grateful for small mercies. Holmes's ordeal (assuming
he were not the murderer) would have been a great
deal more unpleasant if that one had been used. They
would check, of course, but it looked as though Julie
Holmes had been killed with her own knife.

Suicide then? But by stabbing herself (a method
rarely chosen by suicides) and in the hall, by the front
door? And, what was more, dressed to go out? Highly
unlikely, Thanet thought, but then people did sometimes behave in the most incredible, irrational ways.
The possibility would have to be borne in mind, remote
though it seemed.

But her handbag was missing.

A ring at the bell, then. Julie snatches up the
carving knife (!), opens the door (why, if she was afraid?),
mugger grabs handbag, seizes knife, stabs her, departs

with the loot. Oh yes, he told himself sarcastically, very likely. He must stop all this nonsense and get on with the job. "Find anything else?" he said.

"There's this." Lineham pointed to the table on which sat a brown, simulated-leather box some three inches by two. A film of powder indicated that it had already been tested for prints. Nearby was a scrumple of tissue paper. "I found it on the window sill. The paper was in the waste bin."

"Have you opened it?"

Lineham shook his head. "Johnson was still working on it when I went to tell you about the knife."

Thanet picked up the box, pressed the catch. The lid flew open, revealing a white satin lining in which there was a shallow, curved depression. In the lid was printed in black: A. *Mallowby, Jeweller. High Street, Sturrenden.* Thanet glanced at Lineham. "That mermaid brooch she was wearing, do you think?"

"That's what I thought," Lineham said eagerly. "Looks as though the box might have been wrapped in that tissue paper. In which case, he probably gave it to her tonight. The paper was right on top, in the waste bin."

Thanet handed the box over. "Find out. I'm just going to take a look around upstairs."

Lineham nodded and disappeared into the living-room.

Thanet moved quietly up the uncarpeted stairs. There were, he discovered, three bedrooms, two good-sized rooms and one minute one. The tiny one and the bedroom at the back of the house were both stacked haphazardly with a jumble of furniture and unpacked cardboard boxes. Surely, Thanet thought, they ought to have made more progress than this in six weeks? Though Julie Holmes had been out at work all day, he reminded himself.

The third and biggest bedroom, however, showed where the time had been spent. Thanet switched on the light and stood looking about him with surprised interest. The room was carpeted in deep pink and had been freshly papered in a white wallpaper with a delicately pretty design of wild flowers in two shades of pink and a soft green. Curtains of exactly the same design hung at the big bay window.

"Well, well," murmured Thanet, moving further out into the room. The bedspread was white lace over a deep pink backing which accentuated the pattern and along the whole of one wall was ranged a series of units of white furniture—good quality stuff too, Thanet thought, going to take a closer look—two wardrobes with a dressing-table built between them. There was an oval mirror fixed to the wall above the dressing-table. The overall effect of the room was fresh, pretty and strangely impersonal. It looked exactly like a magazine illustration, and was just as lifeless. There were the pretty ornaments, the carefully arranged posy of flowers on the bedside table, the tasteful prints. But there was a complete absence of clutter. The top of the dressing-table was bare, the surface of the twin bedside tables empty save for an alarm clock on one side (his, presumably) and the flowers (hers). There was absolutely nothing visible in the room to reveal the personality of its owners.

The small drawers at the top of the bedside cupboards were slightly more fruitful. In Julie's was a bottle of sleeping tablets and a neatly folded clean handkerchief. In Holmes's was a well-thumbed stack of girlie magazines. Thanet pursed his lips over these, wondering how long the Holmeses had been married. Surely not long enough for him to turn to these, as a substitute for the real thing? Perhaps they were a legacy of Holmes's three months of relative celibacy, Thanet reflected as he carefully replaced them. Or perhaps not. Thanet looked around the room with new eyes. Holmes had, clearly, indulged all his wife's whims to get this room exactly as she wanted it. As a bribe? A distasteful thought, but one to be taken seriously.

Thanet moved across to the dressing-table. The top drawers contained neatly ranged cosmetics, the lower ones tights, underclothes, scarves, sweaters, all clean and carefully folded. The contents of the two wardrobes were much more revealing. Holmes's was almost empty, containing only one suit, two pairs of jeans, a pair of casual trousers, a denim jacket and, on the top shelf, a small pile of underclothes and two sweaters. On the floor were lined up two pairs of suede shoes, one pair of leather, a pair of slippers and some track shoes.

Julie's wardrobe was a very different matter. Thanet whistled softly as the doors slid back to reveal a full rack of dresses, coats, skirts, trousers, all of them good quality and many expensive. Thanet riffled through them, then stooped to examine a purple plastic carrier bag with TOPS in gold lettering on the side. Expensive indeed. Joan had bought an evening dress at TOPS for the first police ball after Thanet had been promoted to Inspector and the memory of the bill had made Thanet wince for months afterwards. It was a gorgeous dress, Joan had looked marvellous in it and he hadn't begrudged a penny of it, but still . . .

He slid the door closed, thoughtfully, and took one last glance about him before making his way downstairs. Holmes, then, had been over indulgent, uxorious. Remembering those magazines the word 'bribe' slid again into Thanet's mind. What had Holmes been trying to buy? Love? Sexual compliance? And if so, how would he have reacted if his wife had continued to reject him, if—remembering that she had evidently been out when she had said that she would be staying at home like a good little wife—he had been supplanted by a rival?

Thanet grimaced. It looked as though this case might be all too predictable.

2

————*——*——*

Something was tickling his nose, tugging at his attention, dragging him up and away from the luxury of sleep. Thanet opened his eyes. Bridget was peering anxiously into his face.

"OK, Sprig," he whispered. "I'm awake. I'll be out in a minute."

Satisfied, she trotted off towards the door.

Thanet, careful of his back, glanced over his shoulder to make sure that Joan was still asleep, then levered himself out of bed.

In the bathroom he splashed his face in cold water, to wake himself up properly before shaving. It had been half past three in the morning by the time he had finished his preliminary report, four by the time he got to bed, and shaving could be a hazardous business when one was still three-quarters asleep. Joan had often tried to persuade him to use an electric razor but he didn't like them. Perhaps he ought to grow a beard? He peered at his narrow, unexceptional face beneath its thatch of thick brown hair, trying to visualise how he would look. Pointless speculation, really. Joan didn't like beards.

By the time he had finished shaving and had cleaned his teeth he was beginning to feel human again. He would shower later, before dressing. He opened the door on to the landing and with perfect timing three-year-old Bridget came out of her room, trailing dressing-gown and slippers. He helped her into them and then,

18

unable to carry her as he usually did because of his back, he took her hand and they tiptoed downstairs to the kitchen.

This was their special time. Making use of Bridget's inbuilt alarm clock which always woke her at half past six, Thanet had instigated this morning routine when Ben was born. It suited everybody. Joan could sleep on a little after night feeding and Thanet was able to spend some time with his daughter. The demands of his work were such that he frequently missed seeing Bridget in the evenings and all too often a week would go by without his having been able to spend more than a few fleeting moments with her. Bridget loved this early-morning time. At this hour Daddy was hers alone, his attention undivided and guaranteed.

Together they had evolved their own ritual, Bridget laying the table with extreme concentration while Thanet made tea and toast and dispensed cereal and fruit juice. After breakfast he would take Joan a cup of tea in bed before the day began in earnest.

"Bridget saw a baby horse yesterday," she announced, when they were settled at the table.

"Oh? That was nice. A baby horse is called a foal. Where was that?"

Bridget's forehead creased while she thought about it. "By the shops," she said triumphantly at last.

Sounded most unlikely, Thanet thought. But why worry? It didn't matter what they talked about as long as they talked, enjoyed each other's company. As Bridget chattered on he watched her indulgently. She had inherited Joan's fair, clear skin and candid grey eyes, her honey-coloured hair. Whereas Joan's was short and curly, though, Bridget's was soft and fine, its silky tendrils brushing her shoulders. She would, Thanet thought, one day be a very beautiful girl.

At this time of day he tried never to think about his work but suddenly Julie Holmes's face was in his mind. She, too, had been a beautiful girl. If anything like that ever happened to Sprig...

"Is your toast nasty, Daddy?"

Thanet realised that he was scowling, relaxed, shook his head. "No, just something I was thinking of. . . ."

Sturrenden was a thriving market town of some 45,000 inhabitants. It lay deep in the Kent countryside, surrounded by some of the finest farmland in the South of England. Cattle and crops, fruit and hops all flourished, feeding the life of the town which was their heart.

In Thanet's opinion Sturrenden had everything: good shops, excellent schools, a plentiful supply of pubs, a number of churches, two cinemas and even, for the culturally minded, a small but first-rate theatre. It enjoyed all the benefits of country living, yet it was only an hour and a half by fast train to London and close enough to the coast to make summer picnics by the sea an attractive proposition.

As he drove to work on this fine May morning he looked about him with satisfaction. Not for him the dirt and grime of the metropolis, thank you very much. The police force in Sturrenden was well manned and, with very few exceptions, people worked smoothly together, which was good both for morale and efficiency.

There was a delay at the bridge and Thanet had time to notice that the flowering cherries along the tow-paths on either side of the river were just coming into bloom. In a couple of weeks he must remember to take Joan on one of their favourite outings, a drive through the orchards at blossom time.

By the time he arrived at the police station, however, his mind was focused firmly on work: first, a quick clearing away of any routine stuff which might have arrived on his desk this morning (fortunately there was nothing particularly time-consuming today), then he would go out to Gladstone Road to see how Lineham was getting on with directing the search of the area by daylight. After that he would return to the office to take a thorough look at the house-to-house reports, which should be typed up by then. And then . . . well, he'd decide later, when he'd seen what had come in.

He was in Gladstone Road by a quarter to nine. Lineham, Carson and Bentley were poking about in the patch of waste land next to the Holmes's house.

"Found anything?" Thanet asked.

Lineham shook his head. "Not a sausage. Except for rubbish, rubbish and more rubbish, of course."

"Have you seen Dobson, the builder, yet?"

"Yes. He came over to speak to us when he opened up the yard. Said we could search it whenever we liked, if we wanted to."

"What's he like?"

"A bit gnome-like. About five two, with a bald head and lots of whiskers."

"Age?"

"Sixty-five or so, I'd say."

"Did he know anything useful?"

"No. The yard opens at eight and the men are sent off to their various jobs. Dobson glimpsed Mrs Holmes once or twice when she left for work, just before a quarter to nine, but he never actually spoke to her. The yard closes at four-thirty, so by the time she got home from work at a quarter to six it would all be shut up."

"Have you seen Holmes this morning?"

"No. He's up, though. The bedroom curtains are drawn back now. Do you want to see him?"

"Not at the moment. I'm going to take a quick look around the other streets back there."

It was a strange district, Thanet thought as he walked, a little world of its own, bounded on one side by the only road into the area, on the second by the railway line, on the third by the narrow band of trees behind the metal fence which Thanet had noticed the previous evening, and on the fourth by a row of shops.

Between Gladstone Road and the shops, and parallel to them, were three cul-de-sacs of mean little back-to-back Victorian terraced houses fronting directly on to the pavements, their back yards divided by narrow alleyways which Thanet certainly wouldn't have cared to use at night. They, too, had been named after nineteenth-century politicians—Disraeli Terrace, Palmerston Row, Shaftesbury Road.

Thanet had no intention of visiting any of the houses as yet, so there did not seem to be much point in walking along one of the cul-de-sacs and back again. It was therefore not until he had returned to Gladstone Road and had gone to take a closer look at the swing gate and the footpath to the station that he made an interesting discovery: glancing to his left he found that the far ends of the cul-de-sacs were linked by a footpath which ran along between the metal fence and the blank sides of the last terraced house in each row.

Access to Gladstone Road was not then, as he had thought, limited to the road way in. The Holmes's house could also be reached by walking along any one of those cul-de-sacs and turning into the footpath which led to the railway station.

Thanet pushed open the swing gate and walked quickly through the narrow copse, emerging at the far end within sight of the station. The strip of trees, he now saw, separated the area of terraced houses from the grounds of a modern factory. He glanced at his watch. Those reports should be ready shortly. He must get back to the office.

He picked up Sergeant Lineham on the way and they both settled down to study the reports in a silence broken only by the little popping noises made by Thanet's pipe, the scrape of a match as he relit it from time to time.

Finally Thanet pushed the papers away from him, sat back. "Television is the policeman's bane," he said. The previous evening most people seemed to have been glued to their sets watching *The Pacemakers*, a new and very successful series which started at eight-thirty and finished at nine-thirty—unfortunately the very period which interested the police. "The report on Mrs Horrocks is interesting, though."

Horrocks was a travelling salesman and the previous evening he had, according to his wife, been "hopping mad." The inhabitants of all those closely packed ter-

raced houses had parking problems. There simply wasn't
enough parking space, and some of the locals had to be
content with leaving their cars in front of the row of
shops, coming to regard certain spaces as theirs by
right.

Horrocks, recently moved into the district, was
one, and he had been incensed to find that on Tuesday
evenings his parking space was frequently purloined by
a green Triumph Stag. Last night had been no exception and every quarter of an hour or so he had gone out
to see if he could catch the intruder and have it out
with him. It had been especially irritating as he had
been due to leave on one of his frequent selling trips up
North—he preferred to do the long haul by night—and
he had been angry at having to spend his last couple of
hours at home in this way. What was more, he had
again failed to catch the owner of the Triumph.

Unfortunately, by the time Thanet's man had called,
Horrocks had already left and although his wife knew
that the Triumph had been there when her husband
had arrived home at a quarter past seven and had still
been there when *The Pacemakers* started at eight-
thirty, she did not know if it had gone by the time
Horrocks left just before nine.

The presence of the Triumph was confirmed by a
Mr Carne, who used the parking space next to Horrocks
and who had noticed it when taking out his own car at
eight o'clock to pick up his daughter from a music
lesson. It had still been there at eight-twenty, when he
returned.

"We'll have to try to trace Horrocks," Thanet said.
"Send the same man—Bentley, wasn't it?—to go and
find out Horrocks's schedule. And to see if he can get
hold of Carne, find out if he can remember any details
of the Triumph's registration number... Interesting,
isn't it? Holmes's night-school evening."

"You think the owner of the Triumph might have
been visiting Mrs Holmes, sir?"

Thanet shrugged. "Who knows? It's worth checking.

Though if he was going to her house, why was she wearing outdoor clothes?"

"Perhaps they went out for a drink?"

"Possibly . . . Then there are these two reports of 'a tall dark man.' No further details. How vague can you get? Seen passing the end of Disraeli Terrace in the direction of Gladstone Road at about a quarter to nine by the woman whose daughter had toothache. Also seen passing Shaftesbury Road in the direction of Gladstone Road by the man who'd been walking his dog, at about twenty to nine, he thinks. Where's that map?"

They bent over it together.

"As I thought," Thanet said. "Disraeli Terrace is nearer Gladstone Road than Shaftesbury Road is. The times should have been the other way around."

"They both say they're not certain of the time. One of them must be a few minutes out."

"Mmm. I think we'd better check on it all the same. And we want more details about our tall dark stranger. Better send Carson. He saw both these witnesses, didn't he? I know he says he pressed them, but they may have remembered something since." Thanet paused, consulted his notes. "And that's about it, isn't it?"

"Sir, what about . . ." Lineham stopped, swallowed.

"What about what?" Dammit, I must be more patient with him, thought Thanet. "Go on," he said, more gently.

"Well, the husband, sir. I know the evidence of his friend seems to let him out, but we don't know, do we? I mean, if he had stabbed her in the instant of opening the door, the friend wouldn't have been any the wiser, would he?"

"The thought had crossed my mind," Thanet said drily, "but at this stage I feel we ought to keep an open mind." His pipe had gone out and he took time to relight it. "For one thing, we ought to wait for the report on the knife, and for the path report. If Holmes did kill her she would have to have died instantly for Byfleet to be so convinced Holmes didn't do it. If there'd been the least sign of life . . . But of course, it's possible that Byfleet is lying to protect Holmes. And then, the whole set-up is peculiar. Stabbing, I always think, is more of an impulse crime. If Holmes had planned to use Byfleet as a witness to prove his innocence, he would not only have had to carry the knife with him to evening class but somehow have had to ensure that his wife was waiting for him at the door."

"He could deliberately have left his key behind so that she would have had to open it."

"Yes, but he couldn't count on her answering at once, could he? She might have been washing her hair or in the bath, then his witness would have been out of sight by the time she opened the door. That swing gate is only about a hundred yards away."

"He could have tried it, then if it didn't work and she didn't answer the door before Byfleet was out of sight, he could have planned to put off killing her to another Tuesday."

"He'd have to be a pretty cold-blooded character," Thanet said grimly. "And as I say, all this planning doesn't fit in with stabbing, to my mind. I could see him killing her in anger, or in a fit of jealously—if he caught her with another man, for instance . . . You saw their bedroom."

"Yes. He was besotted with her, I'd say. All those expensive clothes, and his own wardrobe practically empty."

"I know. So all right, he may have had a motive, there might have been another man . . . She may have gone out to meet him, while Holmes was at night school . . . All the same, I'm not happy about the mechanics of the actual killing. I can't seem to visualise it, somehow. I just don't think we have enough to go on. So we'd better do some digging while we're waiting for the results of the lab tests and path. report. I want you to get along to Homeright, see what you can find out about Holmes, any gossip and so on. Did you manage to get that photograph of Mrs Holmes?"

Lineham took an envelope out of his pocket, extracted the print.

Julie Holmes was leaning against a five-barred gate, gazing solemnly into the camera.

"Holmes says it's a good likeness, sir."

"Good. Get some copies made, then make sure it gets into tomorrow's papers—tonight's, if possible. If she was out last night, someone might have seen her."

Thanet stood up and Lineham followed suit. Watching him, Thanet sensed a certain reluctance. Why...? Suddenly it dawned on him. Lineham was dying to know what he, Thanet, was going to do. Thanet remembered only too well how he'd liked to be kept informed, when he was in Lineham's position. "I think I'll go along and have a sniff around the Estate Agents where Mrs Holmes worked. It's just possible there might be a man there who was interested in her. Or perhaps there'll be other girls who might have picked something up."

He had been right. Lineham made for the door with alacrity now. Thanet was about to follow him when the phone rang.

"Thanet here."

The fingerprints on the knife had been Julie's. Some were blurred but they were indisputably hers. The written report would follow.

Thanet relayed the information to Lineham, who was hovering at the door.

"Hers!" Lineham's forehead creased as he assimilated this interesting piece of information. "Still, it's not really surprising, is it? It was her knife, after all. Do you think there's any chance it was suicide?"

"With her coat on? In the hall? I doubt it. I expect Doc Mallard's report will enlighten us. Meanwhile, let's get on. Don't forget to put those enquiries in hand before you go, will you?"

Lineham tapped his notebook. "I've made a list."

Yes, Thanet thought, Lineham would do. He would do very well indeed.

3

Jefferson and Parrish, Estate Agents, occupied choice premises in the High Street. Thanet parked without compunction in the small car park at the rear reserved for clients, noticing with interest a green Triumph Stag in the slot marked Mr J. Parrish. He made a note of the registration number before making his way around to the front of the building.

The clients of Jefferson and Parrish had generously supplied the firm with top-grade wall-to-wall carpeting, a spectacular rubber plant and a receptionist who could have stepped off the cover of a women's magazine. She was not without feeling however; when Thanet introduced himself and stated his errand the girl shivered, grimaced.

"I heard it on the news this morning. I couldn't believe it. Poor Julie. . . ."

"You knew her well?"

"Not really. She'd only been here four or five weeks. All the same, working with someone—"

The buzzer sounded on the girl's desk.

Thanet waited until she had finished with the phone. "What was Mrs Holmes's job here, exactly."

"She was Mr Parrish's secretary." The girl's eyes swerved away from Thanet's.

"Then I'd like to see Mr Parrish, please. Perhaps I could have another word with you afterwards?"

Parrish was tall, dark, of athletic build and had the kind of good looks associated in television advertisements with masculine pursuits such as climbing, sailing, driving fast cars and smoking seductive cigars. He wore a beautifully cut, dark-brown hopsack suit, a cream shirt, a tie diagonally striped in chocolate, cream and coffee and a fawn waistcoat with a brown and red overcheck. The effect—no doubt carefully studied—was conservative with a dash of daring. He would, Thanet thought, be very attractive to women, with that studied charm and low, caressing voice. He also had two characteristics which Thanet disliked: a smile which switched on and off like a neon sign and never reached his eyes, and a habit of saying, "mmm, mmm, mmm" all the while his companion was speaking—intended presumably to convey an impression of intense interest but succeeding only in making Thanet feel that he had to hurry through everything he said.

"A terrible thing," said Parrish when they were seated. "Terrible." Thanet waited.

"I could hardly believe it, when I heard it on the radio this morning. I was shaving." And he turned his head aside with a slight, rueful smile, to show Thanet the little cut on the side of his neck.

Thanet nodded, still saying nothing.

"Well, Inspector," said Parrish, throwing himself back in his chair with an alert, eager movement and spreading both hands palm-downward on the desk before him, "how can we help you?"

Thanet noted the first person plural, the implication that Parrish himself could do nothing of the kind.

"Mrs Holmes was new to the area. This was where she worked. We have to try to find out all we can about her and this seemed the obvious place to start."

"But why? Surely . . . look, didn't it say her body was discovered by her husband, when he got home from night school? Well, I mean, it must have been someone who thought the house was empty, broke in. . . . Mustn't it?"

"At this stage we have to take every possibility into consideration. Now, I understand Mrs Holmes was your secretary. Could you tell me about her?"

"I'm not very good at describing people, I'm afraid," said Parrish.

I bet you aren't, thought Thanet. He guessed that Parrish was too self-absorbed to take in much of other people.

"I get on well with them, of course, you have to, in this job, but... well, Ju... Mrs Holmes... Oh, what the hell, I called her Julie, of course, this is a small office and she was my secretary, after all. Well, she was very quiet, reserved. Didn't have much to say for herself. Efficient, though. I rarely had to explain anything twice, or had reason to complain. And that's about it, I suppose."

"Did she get on well with the other girl?"

"Which one?"

"Is there more than one?"

"Yes. There's Maureen Waters—tall, brunette—and Joy Clark. She's a redhead. Wasn't she...? Oh of course, I'd forgotten. Joy's popped along to the printers to pick up some brochures for a client who's coming in later this morning."

"Well, did she? Get on well with them?"

"Oh yes—so far as I know, anyway. You'd better ask them."

"Would you say that Julie Holmes was attractive to men?"

If this question alarmed him Parrish neatly concealed it by leaning across his desk to pick up a cigarette box. "Cigarette, Inspector? No?" He took one himself.

Thanet detected no betraying tremor as Parrish lit up.

"Attractive to men," Parrish repeated thoughtfully, as if the concept were new to him. "Well, I don't know. Yes, I suppose she might have been. She was a very pretty girl, certainly, but of course, she was married...."

"Are you?"

"Married? No, why?"

"Just wondered."

"No, I... well, I suppose I just haven't found the right girl yet. And of course, married women... After all, there're plenty of the other sort around. Why risk getting involved with an enraged husband and so on if you don't have to. . . ."

"Quite. So there was no one special, as far as you know, paying attention to Mrs Holmes?"

"Not to my knowledge, no."

"Mr Jefferson is the only other man here, I gather?"

Parrish gave a snort of genuine amusement. "You're barking up the wrong tree there, Inspector. I don't suppose old Jeff'd notice if Simone Signoret walked stark naked through his office." He sobered down. "Sorry. Look, Inspector, it's a pity I can't help you, but really, there's nothing to tell. Julie Holmes was a nice, quiet, pleasant girl. She got on with the job, gave no trouble, scarcely caused a ripple. I'm sorry about what happened to her, very sorry, but I really don't see what more I can tell you."

"Right." Thanet rose. "But there's just one other question."

"Yes?"

"Last night. Could you tell me where you were between, say seven and nine-thirty pm?"

Parrish's eyebrows swooped into a frown. "Now look here, Inspector, what are you implying?"

"Nothing, nothing at all. But you must see that, as a matter of course, we have to put that question to everyone who had anything at all to do with Mrs Holmes."

Parrish was clearly sceptical. "Well, I suppose there's no harm in telling you. I was at home all evening from about six o'clock. I was bushed, as a matter of fact—had a heavy day yesterday. So I thought I'd stay in, have an early night."

"Is there anyone who can corroborate that?"

"I doubt it. We don't exactly live in each other's pockets."

"We?"

"I've got a flat in Maddison House."

The only block of luxury flats in the district. "You're sure you saw no one, spoke to no one, all evening?"

"I don't think so. No, hang on. I saw Morrison, on my way in. He's the caretaker, lives in the basement with his wife."

"And that would have been at . . . ?"

"About six, as I said."

"Good. Fine." Thanet closed his notebook with a snap. "Well, I won't take up any more of your time, Mr Parrish. Thank you for being so helpful."

"Not at all. Not at all." Parrish accompanied him to the door, effusive now in his relief. "Anything we can do to help. Any time."

"You won't mind my having a word with your receptionist, then?"

"Er . . . no. Not at all." Parrish waved him into the outer office. "Help yourself."

Maureen Waters stopped typing as Thanet approached. She had been crying; her mascara was smudged. He perched on the corner of her desk and smiled down at her encouragingly.

"Tell me about Mrs . . . about Julie," he said.

"D'you think you could sit on a chair? You make me nervous, looming over me like that." She gave an apologetic little laugh.

"Sure." Thanet pulled up a chair, sat down and waited.

"She was very nice. Quiet . . . Good to work with."

"You got on well with her," Thanet encouraged.

"Pretty well, yes. We both did—Joy and I, that is." Maureen hesitated.

"But . . . ?"

She gave him an embarrassed, sideways glance. "Oh, I don't know . . . it seems so awful . . ."

"What does?"

"Well, she's dead. I don't like to say anything that might give you the wrong impression. . . ."

"Look, Miss Waters, I can see you're not a gossip," Thanet said, meaning it. "So if there's anything, anything at all which might help us to undertand Mrs Holmes better . . ."

Maureen sighed. "Yes, of course." Then she went

on hesitatingly, picking her words with care, "It's not that it's anything against Julie, not really. I mean, she seemed unconscious of it. Well, she had this attraction for men, you see. You only had to watch . . . If a male client came into the office . . . I don't want you to think I was jealous . . . no," she said painfully, "that's not true. I was jealous, but only of that . . . power she had, not of Julie herself, if you see what I mean. Well, any girl would be jealous. She didn't even have to make any effort, you see, it just happened. But you couldn't hold it against her because, well, how can I explain, it didn't mean anything to her. She just wasn't interested, really. But that didn't seem to make any difference, to the men, I mean." She stopped, glancing uneasily at Thanet. "It's so difficult to explain."

"You're doing fine. Go on. Tell me a little more about this . . . power she had."

"Well, she was very quiet. Withdrawn. Dreamy. Very attractive, of course. And not shy, exactly, just . . . reserved. She was perfectly fit, physically, so far as I knew, anyway, but she gave the impression of being frail, a bit helpless, I suppose. Anyway, men seemed to go for it—jumped to open doors for her, picked things up if she dropped them . . . sort of hovered around her. I'm a woman and I honestly couldn't see what it was she had, but there was no doubt she had it."

"There's something I must ask, and you might find it difficult to answer," Thanet said. "But please try. Was there anyone, either in the office here or amongst the clients, who showed her special attention?"

Maureen's eyes flickered to the door of Parrish's office and she shook her head, a tight little shake as though she were holding something back with difficulty.

He wouldn't put it past Parrish to have his ear glued to the keyhole, Thanet thought. He'd have to get Maureen out of the office. He glanced at his watch in pretended surprise. "I'm afraid I shall have to go," he said. "Could you walk as far as the car park with me, so that we could go on talking? It would save me time."

"I suppose so." She followed him reluctantly.

Outside he said, "I thought it might be easier for you to talk out here. You didn't really answer my question just now, did you? *Do* you know of anyone who was interested in Julie?"

When she didn't reply he glanced at her. Her mouth was set in an obstinate line. He didn't press her but waited until they had reached the entrance to the car park. Then he stopped, turned to face her. "Look Miss Waters, I'll be frank with you. I think I understand your problem. You have some information which you know I ought to have but something, loyalty I would guess, is holding you back. Am I right?"

She wouldn't look at him.

He tried again. "Put it this way. If it turned out that the person you are reluctant to talk about had killed Julie, would you still want to protect him?"

That shocked her. "No, of course not!"

"And if he didn't, how could anything you say harm him?" His point had gone home, he could tell. He waited a moment longer then went on softly, "It's Mr Parrish, isn't it?"

She hesitated, then nodded miserably, biting her lip.

"Then you really must tell me."

But still she stood silent.

"He was interested in Julie?"

Maureen nodded again then finally made up her mind. "I suppose there's no reason why I shouldn't tell you really, there's nothing much to tell. In fact, that's about it. He was interested in her."

"You mean she didn't respond?"

"No. Not at all, so far as we could tell. Of course, she was married, but Mr Parrish can be very . . . persuasive, when he wants to be."

"He likes women," Thanet prompted.

"Yes. Oh dear, that makes him sound awful, and he's not. He's great fun to be with—yes, I've been out with him, in the past. So has Joy, for that matter. But it was never serious, not with either of us, and we both knew it. And it was ages ago, anyway, months before

Julie came. I think he's had a girlfriend somewhere else, for some time, until Julie arrived. And then, well, I told you, she just had this terrific attraction for men, and I suppose working with her all day . . . It was obvious he'd fallen for her."

"But she didn't respond, you say?"

"No. Not at all."

"How did she react to him, then?"

Maureen shrugged. "She just took no notice of him, when he tried to flirt with her. Just ignored it or, if it was very obvious, brushed it aside."

"And how did he feel about that?"

"Well, he pretended to laugh it off, but he didn't like it, obviously. He's not used to that sort of treatment. He's usually the one who calls the tune."

Maureen obviously had Parrish's measure, Thanet thought. It was interesting, though, that there was no bitterness. "But you're quite sure there was nothing between them?"

"I'd swear to it, yes. And in any case, lately . . ."

"Yes?"

"I'm not sure if I should say this. I might have got quite the wrong impression."

"Go on, please."

"Well, it seemed to me that lately Julie had something else on her mind. Something that was upsetting her. I mean, she was always quiet, like I said, but for the last couple of weeks she's been acting strangely, sort of jumpy. And she's been looking unwell, pale, as if she hadn't had enough sleep."

"But you've no idea what was bothering her, if there was something?"

"None, no."

"Just one other thing. Did anyone here know that Mr Holmes went to night school on Tuesdays?"

"Yes. We all knew. It came up over coffee one day."

"Mr Parrish was there too?"

"Yes."

"Thank you."

*   *   *

Thanet gave a last, thoughtful look at Parrish's car as he drove off. Interesting that the man had pretended not even to have noticed Julie's charms. Guilt, or merely caution? In any case, unwise. He might have guessed the other girls in the office would have noticed his attempts to win her over.

So, some checking was now necessary. Someone would have to go out to Maddison House, to find out if anyone had seen Parrish go out last night. If Bentley had managed to track Carne down, he might perhaps have been able to find out the registration number of that green Triumph. If not, further enquiries would have to be made to find out if anyone else had noticed it. It certainly seemed too much of a coincidence, that Julie's boss should own one.

As he drove, Thanet mused on the possibility of Parrish's guilt, reproaching himself as he realised that he would be quite pleased if Parrish turned out to be the murderer. Really, just because he didn't like the man.. Where's that famous impartiality we're supposed to cultivate, he reprimanded himself. Not to mention the open-mindedness he was always advocating to Lineham.

The preliminary path. report was awaiting him and after despatching someone to Maddison House he skimmed through it eagerly, then read it again more slowly, twice. Julie had been stabbed in the heart, but in such a way that it was difficult to tell whether death had been instantaneous or whether she might have lived for some minutes afterwards. Why should there be any doubt on that point? Thanet wondered furiously. Surely they should have been able to tell? But in his experience Mallard was meticulous in his work. Thanet would raise the question next time he saw the pathologist but meanwhile he would just have to accept his findings. So, Thanet thought ruefully, bang goes any neat elimination of Holmes.

The report went on to say that the entry to the

wound was slightly ragged and the angle such that it could not have been self-inflicted. There was bruising on the back of both her hands, too.

Thanet laid the report on his desk, sat back and thought. Not suicide, then. Julie had been holding the knife, but had not killed herself. The bruising confirmed that there had been a struggle. Had she picked it up to attack someone, or to defend herself?

Try as he would, Thanet couldn't visualise the quiet Julie lying in wait for her husband with a carving knife. Nor, for that matter, could he see Holmes calmly taking the knife to night school with the intention of killing her when he got home. Yet if he were guilty, it couldn't have been any other way, there wouldn't have been time, with only those fifteen or twenty seconds to play with. In any case, it was Julie's prints that were on the knife—and not only on it, Thanet discovered, glancing at the written report which had now come in—but superimposed on many others in such a position as to indicate that she had been holding the knife as a dagger, not as a breadknife. Was it possible that Holmes could have killed her, that when she was dead he had simply taken her hand and pressed it around the dagger, holding it in the right position to give the impression she had been gripping it herself? He must ask Doc Mallard. But again, would there have been time? Thanet honestly could not see that there would. And in any case, his original objection still held: he could see Holmes driven into a stabbing, committing the crime on impulse in a fit of jealous rage, perhaps, but this way? Unconsciously he shook his head. It just didn't feel right.

Then, too, there was the question of why Julie had been dressed to go out.

No, he would guess that there must have been a quarrel. Not with Holmes, of course, but with someone else. He closed his eyes, tried to visualise the scene. Julie is either about to go out with someone or has just arrived home with him. In any case, she is wearing her brown tweed coat, the mermaid brooch on her lapel.

They quarrel. Perhaps the atmosphere has been building up between them for some time. Finally it erupts
into violence. He threatens her, she becomes frightened.
They are in the kitchen and she snatches up the carving
knife, runs into the hall. He follows, tries to take the
knife away and in the ensuing struggle she is killed. She
falls. He panics and runs, having enough presence of
mind, however, to take her handbag in order to try to
make it seem that she had been killed by an intruder.
The struggle must have been brief, the murderer gloved;
despite an exhaustive search nothing had been found
that could lead to an identification of the killer.

Thanet gave a slow nod of satisfaction. Yes, this was
a much more feasible reconstruction of what had
happened. Gradually, now, he was feeling his way closer
to the truth. Proving it, of course, was quite another
matter. Thanet turned back to his desk.

During the next hour information began to trickle
in. First, Lineham arrived to report on his visit to
Homeright. Holmes had not gone into work this morning and Lineham had been able to question people
without the embarrassment of having him around.
Holmes, it seemed, was fairly popular at the supermarket.
He was efficient, good at dealing with the staff and the
only criticism seemed to be that he was somewhat
over-ambitious. "On his way up," as they put it, Lineham
said. "Personally I think comments like that have arisen
from jealousy. I gathered that at twenty-five Holmes is
one of the youngest managers in the chain." There were
no whispers of any involvement with another woman
and the consensus of opinion was that he was too fond
of his wife for there to have been any possibility of one.

Next the phone rang with the information that
Julie's handbag had been found in the dustbin of the
end house in Disraeli Terrace. Refuse was collected in
that area on Wednesdays and a dustman who had heard
the news of Julie's death on the radio that morning had
recognised the importance of his find and had handed it
in.

Thanet had the bag sent up and examined its

contents; the wallet section of Julie's purse was empty. Holmes confirmed that it should have contained at least five pounds in notes, the remnants of the previous Friday's house-keeping money. The murderer, then, had had enough intelligence to carry through his plan of deflecting suspicion on to a house-breaker. Thanet was still not inclined to believe that she really had been killed by a thief; past experience had taught him otherwise. He could not yet, however, entirely dismiss the idea.

The next report came from the man who had been sent to check on Parrish. There was apparently nothing to prove or to disprove Parrish's claim that he had spent the previous evening in his flat. The caretaker confirmed that he had seen Parrish arrive home at about six, but he and his wife had gone out to visit a married daughter shortly afterwards, and no one else had seen Parrish all evening. His neighbours had been cooperative but unhelpful.

"Keep asking," Thanet said.

Thanet and Lineham were still discussing Parrish when the phone rang again. Lineham could see the interest which sparked in Thanet's face as he listened. Thanet scribbled and put the phone down with an air of satisfaction. "Bentley," he said. "Something positive at last. Carne remembered the letters of the registration number on that green Triumph—GKP—because of some personal association. They match the letters on Parrish's Triumph. It's not enough, of course, for a positive identification, but I think we can try a bit of bluff." He looked at his watch. "He's probably out at lunch at the moment. We'll have a sandwich at the pub, then go and see if he can wriggle out of this one."

4

Parrish was clearly none too pleased to see Thanet back so soon. "I was just leaving, to show a client over a property. It's an important sale, so I hope this won't take long."

"I shouldn't think so, sir," said Thanet pleasantly. "There are just one or two small points..."

Parrish did not invite them to sit down and remained standing himself, as if to emphasise that the interview would be brief.

"If we could sit down...?" Thanet said.

"Help yourself," said Parrish ungraciously and sat down behind his desk with an air of resignation.

"Now, about last night," Thanet began, pretending to consult his notes, "you say you were at home all evening?"

"I *was* at home all evening."

"And you're quite sure that there is no one who can corroborate this? Please," Thanet said, holding up a hand as Parrish opened his mouth, obviously to protest, "do give the matter some thought. It really is very important."

"No," he said, "there's no one. But then, why should there be? I live alone, as I told you, and unless I'm entertaining there rarely is anyone who could confirm that I'm there."

"No phone calls from friends?"

Parrish thought again, shook his head.

Thanet sighed. "Where do you keep your car, Mr Parrish?"

39

"In a lock-up garage at the back of the flats. There's a block of them, for residents." Parrish shifted slightly in his chair. "Look here, Inspector, what is all this about?"

"And last night your car was in your garage?"

"Of course."

"Then perhaps you could explain," Thanet said softly, "how it is that we have two independent witnesses who swear that your car was parked last evening in front of the shops in Parnell Road?"

Parrish stared at him without expression for a few minutes and then, lifting his hands in a gesture of submission, said with a rueful smile, "All right, Inspector, it's a fair cop, as they say. I give in. Yes, I was out last evening, my car was parked in Parnell Road, and if you want to know why I didn't say so before, it's because there was a lady involved. She's married, and I didn't want to embarrass her."

"I thought you made a point of avoiding married ladies, sir?"

"Fate occasionally pushes one in my direction. It's unfortunate, but it happens, and of course, when it does, discretion is called for."

"But why not tell me this morning? Why bother to lie?"

Parrish shrugged. "I suppose, because if one does have an affair with a married woman, one gets into the habit of trying to keep it quiet, even in these rather unusual circumstances. Also, I was trying to spare the lady. I knew that if I told you the truth, you would be bound to want to check with her."

"So your lying had nothing to do with the fact that your car was parked only a few minutes walk from Mrs Holmes's house?"

Parrish sat up with a jerk. "Only a few minutes from . . . My God. I had no idea."

"You really didn't know that she lived quite close to Parnell Road?"

"Of course I bloody didn't. If I had, I'd have told

you straight off where I was last night, instead of giving you reason to get suspicious of me!"

"So you won't mind, in the circumstances, giving us the name and address of this . . . lady."

"Certainly not. It's Phyllis Penge. 14, Palmerston Row. She'll confirm everything I told you."

"And you arrived at her house at . . . ?"

"Not at her house, Inspector. At my flat. We might as well get it straight this time. I've got a flat over one of the shops in Parnell Road. I've had it for about three years now. It's very small, but quite useful."

"Useful?"

"I use it to entertain my mistresses."

"Why a second flat, when you have a perfectly good one already? It's not as if you were married."

Parrish shrugged. "Shall we say I find it easier not to get too, well involved, when they don't know where I live. Which is especially important when a jealous husband is involved."

"I see." Thanet was finding it difficult to hide his distaste. He was, however, not here to make moral judgements. "So this flat is where, exactly?"

"Over the last shop in Parnell Road—the one at the far end of the row."

Right next to that convenient footpath leading to Gladstone Road, Thanet thought with a lurch of excitement. His face, however, remained impassive. "And you arrived there at what time?"

"About ten past seven."

"And Mrs Penge?"

"A few minutes later."

"Parnell Road and Palmerston Row are next to each other. Wasn't it a little . . . difficult for Mrs Penge, living so close to your meeting place?"

"Not at all, Inspector. Quite the contrary in fact. It was very handy. Phyllis lives in the last but one house in Palmerston Row. An old lady who is deaf and near-blind lives in the last one. Phyllis just slips out, goes along that convenient footpath and into the entrance to my flat."

So Parrish knew about that footpath. Would Parrish have mentioned it, if he were guilty? If he were clever enough, possibly. "You meet when, usually?"

"Always on Tuesday evenings. Phyllis's husband plays in a darts team on Tuesdays."

"And you've known each other how long?"

Parrish thought. "Three months or so. I bumped into her one evening when I was coming out of the flat. I was alone—I'd stayed behind to straighten things up a bit. I do from time to time."

"After a previous rendezvous, you mean?"

"That's right, Inspector. As it happened, that affair was winding down anyway, so it was very convenient, walking into Phyllis like that." Parrish was leaning back in his chair, thumbs hooked behind lapels, a reminiscent smile on his face. Clearly, he enjoyed his image of himself as The Great Lover.

"Does either of the girls here know about the flat?"

Parrish's smile disappeared. "Good God no. I've taken them both out, but only casually. I've enough sense to keep my love life out of the office."

"And you say you had no idea that Julie Holmes lived in the same area as your flat?"

"No. No idea at all. Why should I? I expect the address is on file, but I couldn't tell you where any of the staff live."

"Gladstone Road was mentioned on the radio, this morning, when Julie Holmes's murder was reported."

"Was it? I didn't notice. I was too shaken by the news to take in the details."

"How long did you and Mrs Penge stay in the flat?"

"Until about half past nine. At least, she left at half past, I stayed on for a few minutes afterwards, to tidy up. In any case, as she lives so close we always leave separately. I don't suppose anyone's ever seen us together."

"I see." And he did, only too well. If Parrish's mistress confirmed these times, Parrish was well in the clear. Thanet's voice remained cheerful however as he said, "Well, I think that's all for the moment, Mr

Parrish." He and Lineham stood up. "I do wish, though, that you'd told me all this this morning. It would have saved us considerable time and trouble."

"I do realise that." Parrish was all contrition. "I apologise, Inspector, I really do. Er . . . You will be discreet, when you question Phyllis?" he went on anxiously, following them to the door. "Her husband . . . I wouldn't like him to . . ."

"Find out that his wife is unfaithful? No, I can quite understand that, Mr Parrish." Deliberately, however, Thanet withheld any such assurance. "That'll give him a few nasty moments," he said grimly as they walked to the car park, "wondering if we're going to spill the beans. No question, was there, of protecting her once he realised his own neck was on the block?"

"Inspector!"

Thanet turned. A red-haired pocket Venus was running towards them, a somewhat hazardous undertaking in that tight skirt and those high heels, Thanet thought. He was right. Just as she reached them she stumbled and was caught by Lineham, who steadied her until she regained her balance. Lineham, Thanet noticed with amusement, was looking somewhat pink about the ears. He turned to the girl. "Miss Clark, I presume?"

"Yes, that's right. Mrs Clark, actually." She was out of breath. "How did you know?"

"Mr Parrish described you to me this morning."

"Oh." Now it was Joy Clark's turn to blush. She quickly recovered herself, however. "I'm Mr Jefferson's secretary and I was in his office when you came just now. Maureen told me I'd missed you. So I thought I'd better come after you."

"There's something you wanted to tell me?"

"Yes." She glanced uneasily at Lineham, who took the hint.

"I'll go on to the car, sir . . ."

She waited until the sergeant was some yards away, then said, "It's about Julie, Inspector. I hope I'm not speaking out of turn, but, well, Maureen told me the sort of thing you were asking her about this morning, and when she said she'd told you she thought Julie'd been a bit jumpy lately, I suddenly realised I might know why." She stopped.

"Yes? Do go on."

"Well, I haven't told Maureen, because it's not something I'm very proud of, it's not the sort of thing you broadcast, but, well, Derek—that's my husband— and me, we haven't been getting on very well lately and in the end we decided to go to Marriage Guidance." She had been gazing down at the ground, describing tiny arcs on the ground with the toe of one dainty shoe and now she glanced up at Thanet as if to gauge his reaction. Apparently reassured she went on, "Well the long and the short of it is that one evening when we had an appointment, we saw another couple come out of the Marriage Guidance premises. It was Julie and her husband."

"You've met him?"

"Yes, once."

"And you're quite certain it was they."

Joy's beautiful copper hair bounced as she nodded vigorously. "Oh yes, absolutely."

"Well thank you, Mrs Clark."

"I didn't know if I ought to tell you or not . . ."

"Every scrap of knowledge helps," Thanet said, giving her the reassurance she obviously needed. "Thank you again. And if you think of anything else . . ."

In the car he relayed their conversation to Lineham.

"So there *was* something wrong between Holmes and his wife," Lineham said.

"Looks like it. I don't see how it alters the situation as far as the murder's concerned—all the arguments against Holmes being guilty still hold. All the same, I think I'll go and have a word with him. You can drop me there and go and see Parrish's mistress. Pick me up when you've finished."

"You think Parrish is in the clear, now?"

Thanet shrugged. "Difficult to tell. If he's telling the truth then obviously he must be. Question the girl closely. Make sure she has plenty of opportunity to trip herself up." Thanet experienced a twinge of doubt. Ought he to go and question the girl himself? But he couldn't go back on his instructions now. His reason would be too obvious. In any case some work must be delegated and Lineham was a good man. He'd surely know if the girl was lying.

Thanet had to knock a second, then a third time before he heard shuffling footsteps in the hall and Holmes opened the door. The man was a mess. He was unshaven, the shadows beneath his eyes were so marked that they looked like bruises and he was wearing the same clothes as the previous evening. He probably hadn't taken them off, Thanet thought; he caught a sour whiff of stale sweat and unwashed flesh as Holmes stood back and without a word gestured to him to come in.

Holmes led the way through the hall, carefully walking around the chalk marks on the floor and almost kicking over a large, flat package leaning up against the wall. He stooped to steady it, then preceded Thanet into the living-room where an atmosphere thick with smoke and an ashtray piled high with cigarette stubs showed how he had spent the day. He collapsed rather than sat in one of the big armchairs, his body automatically assuming lines of hopelessness—head drooping, hands limply upturned on his lap, legs outstretched. He looked, Thanet thought, crushed, defeated.

Thanet came straight to the point. "I understand that you and your wife had been consulting a Marriage Guidance Counsellor," he said.

Holmes shook his head in disgust, reached for yet another cigarette. "My God," he said, "you lot do enjoy digging up the dirt, don't you?" Then, when Thanet made no comment, "Well, what of it?"

Thanet sighed. "Look Mr Holmes, in circumstances like these it is our duty to try to find out everything, and I mean everything, about the people involved. Contrary to what you may believe, we don't enjoy this digging, as you call it, but it has to be done. And until we have found out who killed your wife we have to investigate every scrap of information that comes our way."

The brief spark of belligerence had already died out of Holmes's eyes. His head sagged against the back of his chair. "Oh, what the hell," he said. "What does it matter, now, anyway? Ask away, if you must."

"I'd prefer you to tell me."

Holmes shrugged. "There isn't much to tell." He sat up, lit another cigarette from the butt of the one he had been smoking. "Yes, Julie and I went to see a counsellor—we were supposed to be going again tonight, as a matter of fact. She's . . . she's very kind, very understanding. You feel you can talk to her and she won't come all moral on you."

"What's her name?"

"Mrs Thorpe."

"Go on."

Holmes frowned, looked thoughtfully at his cigarette. "Well, we've been what, five times altogether, I suppose." He stopped.

Thanet sighed inwardly. It looked as though he was going to have to drag the information out of Holmes bit by bit. "You went together each time?"

Holmes cast a quick, wary glance at Thanet as if trying to gauge how much he knew. "We went four times together and Julie went once by herself, the time before last."

"Why was that?"

"Why was what?"

"Why did she go by herself that time?"

Holmes's lips tightened. "She wanted to."

"Any particular reason?"

"Not to my knowledge."

But he was lying, Thanet was certain of it. "Was it prearranged?"

"What?"

"That she should go alone," Thanet said patiently.

"No, she just decided."

"When?"

"The day before we were due to go."

"And you went how often?"

"Once a week."

"Always on Wednesday?"

"Yes."

"So that day, the day when she suddenly decided she wanted to go by herself, would have been a Tuesday, the Tuesday of the week before last, in fact."

Holmes thought. "I suppose so, yes."

"And you really have no idea what made her want to go alone?"

"I told you, no."

Thanet tried another tack. "You must have started going soon after you moved here."

Holmes made a sour face. "That's right. I'd hoped . . . Oh, it was stupid of me, I can see that now, to think the move would make any difference. Places don't really matter, do they, people don't change? Anyway, I didn't realise that then, but when I saw things weren't any better I persuaded Julie to come to Marriage Guidance with me. She hated the idea at first, but once we'd been, well, she liked Mrs Thorpe and I began to hope we might get things sorted out."

Poor beggar, Thanet thought, watching him. Suspect or no, the man was suffering, would go on suffering for a long time to come, by the look of it. He hated putting the next question. "What, exactly, was wrong between you?" he asked.

Holmes shook his head, "Sorry, it's no go. I'm not talking about my private affairs to anybody else. It was bad enough going to Marriage Guidance, to begin with, anyway, so no thank you. I don't care what you think. And I can't see that it matters much."

"Would you have any objection to my going to see Mrs Thorpe?"

Holmes hesitated. "I suppose not. Even if I said yes, I did object, you'd probably go anyway, and that'd put Mrs Thorpe in a fix. They won't discuss clients without their permission. And she's been very good to us . . ."

Mrs Thorpe must be a very special person, Thanet

thought, if at a time like this Holmes could set aside his own feelings out of consideration for her. "Look Mr Holmes, I don't want to interfere, but I'm sure it's not good for you to be alone just now. Isn't there anyone around here you could go to, or who could come and stay with you?"

"I notice you don't suggest I get away for a while," Holmes said bitterly. "Not that there's anyone to go to. Julie's mother is dead and I never got on with my parents, so this is hardly the time to go running home to mum."

"Oh I don't know. It might be the best possible time," Thanet said. "Parents often turn up trumps at a time like this. I've seen it happen."

"Not my parents, believe me," Holmes said.

Thanet stood up. "What about going to a hotel for a few days?" But even as he spoke he knew that this was a fatuous suggestion. If he were in Holmes's position he would just want to crawl away into a corner and lick his wounds for a while before he could feel ready to face the world again.

Holmes shook his head stubbornly. "I'm all right here."

Thanet hesitated a moment longer. But what could he do? "I'll find my own way out," he said.

Lineham was already waiting for him in the car. "No joy," he said. "She was out at work. A neighbour said she won't be home until five-thirty. Apparently she works mornings on Mondays and Fridays, all day Tuesday, Wednesday and Thursday. I'll go back later."

"What time does her husband get home?"

"A quarter past six on the dot, the neighbour said."

"Try to make sure you leave before he arrives." Thanet was feeling depressed after the interview with Holmes. "We don't want to make trouble for them unnecessarily."

"Where now, sir?"

"Back to the office, I think. I'm going to try to get hold of the Holmes's Marriage Guidance Counsellor."

This, however, proved impossible, as the only number in the book for the Marriage Guidance Council was switched into an Ansaphone service and Thanet had to be content with leaving a message.

"You don't look very cheerful." It was Mallard, peering at Thanet over his half-moon spectacles. "Back still bothering you?" he enquired gruffly.

"Oh hullo, Tom. Sit down. No," said Thanet in surprise, "as a matter of fact it's not. Today's the first day when I haven't been conscious of it more or less all the time."

"So why the long face? Didn't you like my beautiful report?"

"It may have been beautiful to you, but it certainly wasn't beautiful to me."

"What did you expect? Cast-iron evidence of who killed her?"

"Certainly."

The two men grinned at each other.

"No, seriously, though," Thanet said, "it wasn't exactly helpful. Except that it does seem certain she didn't kill herself."

"Right. Physically impossible, with the knife at that angle."

"And it definitely was that knife, that killed her?"

"You're thinking it might have been substituted for the real murder weapon? No, no question of that. If there had been, it would have been in my report. That was the knife, all right."

"But there was a slightly ragged entry wound. A struggle, you think?"

Mallard nodded. "The bruises on the backs of her hands bear it out."

"They couldn't have been made by the murderer pressing her hands around the handle of the knife in the hope of making it appear suicide?"

"No."

"The devil of it is," Thanet said, getting up and moving across to the window, "there's so little evidence. Nothing under her fingernails, for instance." There was the hint of a question in the inflection of his voice and Mallard glanced up sharply.

"If there had been, it would have been in the report," he said huffily.

"Of course, Tom." Thanet hastened to reassure him. "You are nothing if not thorough, I know that."

"He was probably wearing gloves," Mallard said. "And the struggle might have been very brief. The girl was no heavyweight, it wouldn't have taken much to overpower her."

"Then there's this question of whether she died instantly," Thanet said.

"Yes, unfortunate, that—that we can't be more definite. Mind, she wouldn't have lingered long. A few minutes, no more."

Enough to clear Holmes, Thanet thought. "But why the doubt?" he asked. "I thought it was always possible to tell, after a post mortem."

"Not necessarily. How the victim died, yes, but not how long it took. Let me explain. In this particular case the point of the knife pierced the pericardium—in layman's terms, the coating of the heart. Now if such a puncture is of sufficient dimensions, death is instantaneous. If, however, it is very small, only slight bleeding may occur at first. But the pressure of each successive pulsation of the heart increases the size of the wound until, bingo, suddenly the pericardium ruptures and there is a massive haemorrhage and death occurs. The point is that when this happens the pericardium tears and so in a post mortem it is impossible to tell whether or not the wound was sufficiently lethal to cause death at the moment of penetration, or whether its size was increased after a delay of some minutes."

"I see." Thanet thought for a while, absorbing the implications of this information. "Some minutes, you say. The time could vary?"

"Oh yes. Depending on the size of the initial puncture and also on what the victim was doing. If he was lying down, the heart would not be labouring as much as if he were standing up, or doing something even more energetic."

"Like struggling?"

"Yes, like struggling. So, yes, as you imply, in this case death would have been accelerated."

"So it is still just possible that her husband could have done it?"

"Frankly, I doubt it, in view of various other factors—none of which, I freely admit, enters my province. And I certainly don't think you could ever take it to court unless you had some other pretty conclusive evidence. A good defense counsel would make mince-meat of you on the medical evidence."

"Quite," Thanet said gloomily.

"Ah well, time I was on my way. Cheer up, Luke. At the moment you look as though you ought to be parading up the High Street with a sandwich board proclaiming *The End Of The World Is Nigh.*"

Thanet gave a shame-faced grin as he said, "Thanks for the explanation, anyway," and saw Mallard to the door.

Returning to his desk he skimmed quickly through the messages which he had pushed aside to ring the Marriage Guidance Council. The two witnesses who had seen the tall dark man walking in the direction of Gladstone Road had had nothing to add to their statements. Both said that their estimate of the time could have been out by a few minutes either way.

Bentley had been unable to get a detailed itinerary of Horrocks's sales trip either from the man's wife or from his firm; the former didn't know it, the latter said that they left such details entirely to their representatives. The best they could do was to provide a list of the towns which Horrocks would be visiting during the time he was away.

Negatives, negatives, negatives. There was nothing constructive, at the moment, that he could do. Thanet glanced at his watch. Six-fifteen. Lineham should soon be reporting on his visit to Parrish's mistress. But apart from that . . . to hell with it, thought Thanet. What was the point in hanging about here beating his brains out for nothing? If he was needed, they knew where to find him. He'd just wait for Lineham's call, then he'd go home. He knew from past experience that this was probably the most constructive move he could make at the moment. Let things simmer for a while, try to put the case out of his mind, come back to it fresh tomorrow.

Lineham rang a few minutes later. Phyllis Penge had confirmed Parrish's account of their meeting in every detail.

"What's she like?" Thanet asked.

"Younger than I'd expected. Lush, sexy type."

"Was she telling the truth, that's the point?" Thanet was aware of a feeling of unease, but couldn't put his finger on its source.

"Oh yes, I'm sure of that. She's not very bright. I don't think she could have been convincing enough if she'd been lying."

"Good," Thanet said, thinking that the news was anything but. "Well, you get off home now, Mike. Get a good night's sleep. We could both do with it."

He replaced the receiver thoughtfully. What was it, just now . . . ? But it was no use, it wouldn't come and he felt more depressed than ever. Parrish was out, then. Now what?

Home, he reminded himself.

It was healing to unlock his front door and hear the normality of splashings and squeals of delight from upstairs.

"Is that you, darling?" Joan appeared at the top of the stairs, face flushed from bending over the bath.

"Daddy!" Bridget appeared beside Joan, dressed only in pants and socks. She flew down the stairs to hurl herself at him.

Thanet grinned up at Joan. "This one hasn't had her tub yet, I gather?"

"No. I'm just finishing Ben."

"I'll do Sprig, then. Come on, young lady." Thanet stooped to pick her up, just remembering his back in time. Better not risk it. He took her hand instead.

After supper Thanet helped Joan to wash up, then left her to make coffee while he selected a record. Bach's double violin concerto, he decided. It had a quality of certainty, of sureness and order which he needed tonight. When Joan came in she settled herself on the carpet at his feet, leaning back against his knees. Thanet stroked her hair, reminding himself thankfully that even if his work was going badly he always had this to come home to. He had a sudden, disconcerting picture of Holmes sunk in his armchair with the overflowing ashtray at his side, his house empty and silent, his much-loved wife dead and even his memories of her tainted by discord. By comparison he, Thanet, was rich beyond telling.

"Do you think . . . ?" he said softly.

Joan twisted her head to look up at him, smiling. "Just what I was thinking," she said.

He stood up, put out a hand to help her to her feet and softly, so as not to wake the children, they went upstairs together.

5

Julie Holmes's photograph appeared in the newspapers next morning and at once the usual flood of telephone calls began: she had been seen in places as far apart as Edinburgh and Penzance and engaged in every activity from roller-skating to prostitution. With their customary resignation Thanet and his team began checking the more likely sightings; one never knew when one might strike gold.

Thanet began ringing Sturrenden Marriage Guidance Council at regular intervals, but it was not until nine-thirty that the Ansaphone service was replaced by the secretary's voice and Thanet discovered that setting up an interview with Mrs Thorpe would not be as easy as he had expected.

It wasn't as though the secretary was rude or difficult, quite the contrary. She was polite, charming even, but adamant. She quite understood the circumstances, she said, and appreciated Thanet's need to see Mrs Thorpe, but she couldn't possibly release Mrs Thorpe's telephone number or make an appointment for Thanet to see her without clearance from Rugby.

"Rugby?" queried Thanet.

"Our headquarters."

"Couldn't you get Mrs Thorpe to ring me, then?"

"I'm sorry. But in circumstances like this there is a certain procedure we have to follow, to protect the confidentiality we promise our clients."

"But there's no question of breaking confidentiality here. Mr Holmes has agreed to my talking to her."

"Yes, I do understand. But I have to check, nevertheless. I'm sorry, Inspector, but I'm only doing my job. I do realise the urgency of your problem, though, and I promise that I will ring Rugby straight away and let you know the moment I have a decision."

And with this Thanet had to be content. The girl, however, kept her word; at ten o'clock she rang back to say that Mrs Thorpe could see him at one, at the M.G.C. premises.

"No earlier?"

"I'm sorry. Mrs Thorpe is counselling all morning."

"Right. One o'clock, then. Thank you."

Frustratingly, it was just as he was leaving, at twenty to one, that the most interesting event of the morning occurred: a phone call from a man called Burt, landlord of the Dog and Whistle in Sturrenden, claiming that on the evening she died Julie Holmes had visited his pub with a man. They had, he said, been in several times before, and he was certain that it had been she.

"You're in luck, Mike. You can get a good pint at the Dog and Whistle. Get over there and we'll meet back here afterwards. I've a feeling this interview with Mrs Thorpe might take some time."

As he drove through the lunch-hour traffic Thanet wondered if he was wasting his time. Wouldn't it have been more sensible to go to the Dog and Whistle with Lineham? The landlord's story certainly seemed the most promising lead they'd had so far. Having been so insistent over the need for the interview with Mrs Thorpe, however, he felt morally obliged to turn up. And, he had to admit it, he *wanted* to see her.

Why?

Well, partly because he genuinely felt that in a case like this, where there was a lack of material evidence, it was the job of the investigating officer to find out as much as he could about the character and life of the victim in the hope that this knowledge might lead him to the murderer, and also because, if he were honest with himself, Julie herself was beginning to intrigue him. He had now spoken to a number of people who had been close to her in her everyday life—her husband, her boss, the girls with whom she worked, and so far she still remained a shadowy figure to him, elusive. She must have trusted Mrs Thorpe, to have asked for an interview alone with her, and Thanet was hoping that she might have confided in her.

Thanet wondered what the counsellor would be like. What sort of a person would want to hear about other people's marriage problems? Thanet's own work was often depressing enough, but the thought of sitting listening to accounts of other people's misery day in, day out, made him shudder.

In the event, Mrs Thorpe was a surprise. She was in her early thirties, small—not much more than five feet—and very slim. She had a mop of dark, curly hair, wore an enormous pair of tinted spectacles and was dressed in faded jeans and a loose overblouse in some soft, blue material.

The counselling room, too, was a surprise. Thanet didn't know quite what he had expected, but it certainly wasn't this small, pleasant sitting-room furnished with comfortable armchairs.

"Do sit down, Inspector," she said. Then she grinned. "I'm not what you expected," she said.

"Is it so obvious?"

"I'm used to it. I'm not quite sure what people expect when they come here, but I suspect it's someone rather staid, elderly and drab." She shrugged. "Still, it doesn't seem to matter what image they start off with. Once you've been with them a short while then you're 'My counsellor' and that's it." She looked at him expectantly and said, "Now tell me how you think I can help you, Inspector. It was a dreadful shock to me, of course, to hear about Julie and anything I can do . . . I'm sorry there was some delay in fixing this appointment, but we simply have to watch this confidentiality thing. If we didn't, people would never feel free to talk to us. D'you know, once a counsellor was called as a witness in a defended divorce case. Her client didn't want her to give evidence and she went to the court with her suitcase packed, ready to go to jail rather than break his confidence."

"What happened?"

"Fortunately she wasn't called! Of course, that's an extreme case, but we really do regard it as a very important rule. So when you rang, naturally our secretary had to get clearance from the powers that be. And check with John Holmes, of course, that he had in fact given his permission for the interview."

"But I told her he had."

"We had to be sure." She grinned again at the look on his face. "I don't suppose you're used to people checking up on you!"

True, he'd experienced a momentary spurt of anger at the idea, but then he realised that this was unjustifiable. If it had been his marriage which was under threat of being exposed to a third party, he would have been glad to know it was protected so carefully. He said so.

"Good," Mrs Thorpe said briskly. "And now . . . ?"

There was silence as Thanet marshalled his thoughts. He felt he could trust this woman and decided to be frank with her. "I'll give you the position first," he said.

Briefly, he related the facts of the case and she listened carefully. She sat quite still, according him a quality of attention rare in his experience. People on the whole were far more interested in talking than in listening.

". . . so you see, I'm here because I feel I have to try to find out all I can about Mrs Holmes, in the hope that this might lead me to finding out who killed her. There is one promising lead at the moment, but it might well just peter out, they often do."

"Yes, I see. Well now, perhaps it would be best if I give you a brief account of the Holmes's case and then you can ask questions if you wish. But first, how is John—Mr Holmes—taking it? Hard, I would guess."

"Very hard. He's very depressed, I'd say . . . He

told me he had an appointment with you last night. He didn't turn up, I gather?"

"No. Hardly surprising, in the circumstances... Perhaps I'll give him a ring. It's difficult, isn't it? But it might just help, to talk to someone about it. If he doesn't want to, fair enough."

"At least it might make him feel someone cares. He has nobody, I gather, no one at all."

"I'll do that then." She paused, thinking. "Well, now, let me see. I've seen them five times in all. Four joint interviews and one, a fortnight ago with Julie alone. They've been married for three years and there was trouble right from the start. They came, ostensibly, with a sexual problem. Julie had no interest in sex, and although they made love from time to time there was no enjoyment in it for either of them. I think John hoped that when they moved here, started a new life in a different place, things would be different, but of course they just brought their problem with them and when he saw things weren't improving he persuaded her to come here. He'd been thinking about it for some time, I believe. Anyway, they'd only been in the area for a week or so when they first came.

"The trouble was, of course, that it wasn't just a sexual problem. As so often happens, their sexual difficulties were just a reflection of their day-to-day relationship. Julie... was a very reserved, withdrawn sort of girl and John quite a thrusting, aggressive, masculine type. That surprises you, I see. But you must remember you've seen him only in a state of acute depression."

"True. And I can see that logically you are right. He'd scarcely be the youngest manager in the chain of Homeright's if he weren't pretty thrusting, as you put it."

"Oh is he? I didn't know that. Yes, that is interesting. Anyway, these two types can go well together—the girl likes being dominated, acquiescent—but in this case Julie... well, it seems that she was incapable of any response. It was as if her feelings, her emotions were locked away somewhere inside her, inaccessible to anyone.

And of course the trouble was that someone like John always responds to that sort of reaction by pressing harder, pushing for some kind of response, all the time. Then she withdraws more, like a snail retreating further into its shell, he redoubles the pressure, she withdraws even more and so on. It's a vicious downward spiral, in which the participants are helpless to prevent the situation from becoming progressively worse. In this particular case John's jealousy didn't help, either."

"Was it justified, you think?"

"I can't be sure, of course, but no, I don't think so. I think Julie was as fond of John as she could be of any man. The trouble was, she was incapable of showing that affection in the way which would convince her husband that she did love him, and he therefore tended to suspect that she was as she was only because there was someone else."

"And you're really pretty certain there wasn't? In your own mind, that is?"

"I told you, no." Mrs Thorpe was silent for a moment, thinking, then she added, "Not from Julie's point of view, anyway. I'm not saying there wouldn't have been someone hovering in the wings, ready to snap her up if her marriage went wrong. She was the sort of girl who would be very attractive to the same strong, masculine type as John. She appeared so soft, so gentle and feminine, that they would imagine conquest as inevitable and see resistance only as a challenge."

"No one specific was ever mentioned?"

"No." She sounded doubtful, though. "There was someone in London before they moved down here. Someone who knew her before she was married and wouldn't leave her alone afterwards. John even had a fight with him once, but it didn't seem to put him off. I think it was the main reason why John was so keen to move down here when the opportunity arose."

"It's surprising, in the circumstances, that he left her on her own in London while they were looking for a house down here."

"Well, apparently this other man was abroad at the

time, and this was the only reason why John agreed to the arrangement. And he used to ring her every evening, I gather, and go home at weekends, of course."

"Do you remember this man's name?"

Mrs Thorpe thought for a moment. "I'm not sure . . . it was . . . Kenny, I think. Yes, that's it. Kenny."

"And his surname?"

"I don't think it was ever mentioned."

"I'm sorry, we seem to have wandered somewhat. Do go on."

"Yes, well let me see, what was I saying? Ah yes. They had become locked in this sort of impasse, then, with the situation becoming progressively worse, when they decided to come here. At first we got absolutely nowhere. It's absolutely essential, you see, to have your clients' complete confidence. And Julie, as I've explained, is the sort of person who finds it near-impossible to open up to anyone. She was just beginning to be less wary of me, I felt, when the situation suddenly began to deteriorate in a most unexpected way. Julie began to have nightmares of a particularly frightening kind. That was when she rang up and asked if she could come to see me alone. When she arrived she was in a terrible state—for the first twenty minutes or so she just sat there, shaking. Eventually I managed to get out of her what was upsetting her.

"Apparently, two nights previous to that interview— and regularly since, I might add—she had dreamt that she was in a cage. She was shut in, trying frantically to find a way out, and failing. And then she would become aware that whatever it was she was terrified of was in the cage with her, and that there was no way of escaping it. It was dark, but she knew that it was coming closer, and then, when it was so close that she could feel the heat of its breath on her cheek, she'd wake up. Just talking about it upset her so . . . d'you know, when she'd finished, she rushed off to the cloak-room and was sick, really sick, poor girl. I went after her and I saw . . . .

"I did wonder if perhaps the cage represented how

she felt about her marriage, but that seemed such a glib explanation and I felt there was more to it than that. I tried to find out what could have triggered off the nightmares, but we just didn't get anywhere. To her knowledge she'd never had this particular dream before, though she did admit to remembering creeping downstairs to look for her mother after bad dreams as a child. Later on, after she'd gone, there was one possible explanation which occurred to me. I already knew that Julie had been brought up by her mother—who died about a year ago—because her father had been killed in a car crash when Julie was very small, about three, I think. I wondered if, perhaps, she had been in the car at the time... well, it would have been a terrifying experience for a small child, especially if her father died as a result of the accident. If she'd been trapped in the car, unable to get out..."

"Quite a likely explanation, I should think."

"But why should she suddenly start having nightmares twenty years later? I mean, what could have caused the memories to be... reactivated?"

"Did she have any memories of the crash?"

"Oh no, none. She talked about it as if she'd only heard about it from someone else—her mother, I assumed. She certainly showed no signs of distress when talking about it—though I suppose that's nothing to judge by. If the experience had been as traumatic as all that, then she might well have wiped it out of her mind completely."

"Did you suggest this explanation to her?"

"There was no opportunity. The following time— last week—she and John came together, and she had asked for my assurance that I wouldn't tell him about the nightmares."

"But he must have known she was having them, surely?"

"Yes, but not what they were about."

"I wonder why she didn't want him to know?"

Mrs Thorpe shrugged. "Who can tell? But she didn't, and of course, having promised, my hands were tied." She hesitated, then went on, "I was really worried about her. When they came last week... she looked awful. Very strained, desperate, almost. I'd say she was very near breaking point."

"Breaking point?"

"Well, as I said, she found it very difficult to express her feelings—to talk about them or to show them. The only emotion I ever saw her show was distress, fear, if you like, over this nightmare. And John seemed incapable of understanding what I explained to you just now—that the harder he pressed the more she would withdraw from him, that what he needed to do was to ease up on that pressure, leave her alone, allow her some space in which she could have an opportunity to sort out her problems and perhaps begin to respond to him differently. Though frankly, I don't know if that could ever have happened."

"So you felt that in a way circumstances were combining to push her towards this breaking point, as you call it?"

"Yes, I do. That was why I was very careful indeed not to put any pressure upon her myself. And she did seem to respond to the gentle approach."

"But if there had perhaps been other pressures, about which we know nothing...?"

The counsellor lifted her hands in a gesture of helplessness. "I just don't know."

"Mrs Thorpe, I must ask you this, though I realise that perhaps it is not a fair question. Do you think that she was capable of turning on her husband with a knife?"

She shifted uneasily in her chair, considered. "I'm sorry, I just don't know. Well, yes, I suppose it would have been possible, if he really had put intolerable pressure on her. It could have been some last, desperate defence of her privacy... Once or twice I've seen what happens when people like Julie, people who seem incapable of showing their feelings, have been pushed too far. They lose control completely, become hysterical, incapable of rational behaviour."

"But it would have to have been done in the heat of the moment."

"Oh yes. I'm pretty sure about that. I simply can't see Julie planning a cold-blooded murder. Nor John, either, for that matter."

"Thank you." Thanet stood up. "You really have been most helpful."

As he left he glanced at his watch. Too late, now to get anything to eat in the canteen. On the way back to the car park he called in at a small pub for a beer and a sandwich. The place was almost empty after the lunch-time rush and he was able to settle down in a quiet corner and think in peace.

He felt he now had a much clearer picture of Julie. And he saw her, above all, as frightened. But, of what? Of her husband, of this boyfriend she had been meeting regularly, if the landlord's tale was to be believed, of those nightmares . . . or of herself? Had she sensed that she was being pushed towards that breaking point Mrs Thorpe had mentioned? And had she, the night she died, reached it?

The question, of course, was who had been with her at the time? The obvious choice (if the landlord's story was true) was the man in the pub. In any case, it looked as though her husband was in the clear, as Thanet had thought. For Julie to have cracked, as she did, there must have been some considerable build-up, a protracted quarrel. Holmes had been at night school all evening, had walked home with Byfleet. Those fifteen or twenty seconds were simply not long enough for such a build-up, even assuming that the quarrel had begun before Holmes left at a quarter to seven. No, there had to be someone else involved. Suddenly, Thanet could hardly wait to hear what Lineham had found out. He left his beer half drunk and hurried back to the car.

As soon as Thanet saw Lineham's face he could tell that the sergeant's trip had been fruitful.

"It was her," Lineham said ungrammatically. "That's

definite. The barmaid saw her too and, being a woman, even described what she was wearing—a brown tweed coat with a mermaid brooch on the lapel. She particularly noticed the brooch because she fancied it, asked Mrs Holmes where she'd got it."

"Good." Thanet sat down, took out his pipe, began filling it. "Go on then. Let's hear the details."

It was, according to the landlord, the third or fourth time that Julie and her boyfiend had visited the Dog and Whistle, always on a Tuesday evening. The landlord was certain of this because Tuesday was Darts Match night and the couple always arrived, separately, soon after the match began at eight.

Last Tuesday had been no exception. The man arrived first, ordered drinks for both of them and waited, sitting at the bar because the pub was crowded and there were no tables empty. Julie arrived soon afterwards and shortly after that a table became vacant and they moved—the barmaid remembered this, because of her interest in Julie's brooch and because, practised at interpreting people's moods, she had seen at once that Julie was "uptight," as she put it.

She had therefore kept an eye on them, interested to see what would happen. She was rewarded by signs of a developing quarrel, Julie shaking her head repeatedly and the man becoming more vehement, leaning forward and making angry gestures.

After about half an hour—the barmaid could be no more accurate than that—Julie had jumped up and ran out of the pub "in a real state, hardly knew what she was doing." She had bumped into one of the darts team without apologising, earning herself some "dirty looks." Her companion had sat on for a few minutes, glowering into his glass and had then finished his drink and left.

"They didn't happen to see if he followed her?"

"No. They were very busy and anyway the windows in the Dog and Whistle are high up. The barmaid couldn't have seen without going outside to look and even if she hadn't been busy I don't think she'd have been interested enough to do that."

"You didn't get the name?"

"No. The man wasn't a regular."

"Pity. Still, things are looking up, aren't they? This all fits in beautifully with what I learned from Mrs Thorpe." Thanet gave Lineham an account of his interview with her.

"Yes. I see what you mean, sir. You think this man might have followed Mrs Holmes back to Gladstone Road after the quarrel, started haranguing her again. She grabs the carving knife and in the struggle she gets killed."

"Seems logical, don't you think, in view of what we now know? Fits all the known facts, too. Let me see. If they stayed at the pub for about half an hour, they must have left between, say, half past eight and twenty to nine. You didn't by any chance think to check how long it takes to walk from the Dog and Whistle to Gladstone Road?"

"Six minutes," said Lineham, with justifiable smugness.

"And she died between eight-thirty and nine-thirty . . . Did you manage to get a decent description of the man?"

Lineham opened his notebook but did not, Thanet noticed, do more than glance at it. He had the description off pat. "About five eleven, good, athletic build, springy walk, hair thick, dark brown, cut to just below his ears, eyes possibly brown. Wearing jeans and a brown suede jacket."

"The barmaid?"

Lineham nodded.

"Wish there were more like her."

Lineham grinned. "She said she noticed him particularly because she fancied him. 'Dishy,' she said he was. I think that's why she kept an eye on him and Mrs Holmes. Hoped that if Mrs Holmes ditched him, he might drift in her direction . . . He could be our 'tall, dark man,' sir."

"He could indeed. Though neither of those two witnesses mentioned seeing Mrs Holmes."

"Perhaps he stayed a little way behind her, to give her time to cool off before he approached her again."

"Mmm. Possibly. Now, how to get hold of him . . . I think we'll plump first for his being that former boy-friend of hers in London. Mrs Thorpe said he was a very persistent type. What did she say his name was? Kenny somebody, that's right. Let's go and see Holmes. No doubt he'll be only too delighted to supply us with details."

6

One of Dobson's lorries was backing out of the builder's yard. Thanet and Lineham had to wait until it had completed its manoeuvres and driven off before they could pull in, in front of Holmes's house.

Holmes looked even worse than the previous day. Still unshaven, still wearing the same clothes, he said nothing when he saw the two policemen, simply turned and shuffled into the living-room, once again carefully avoiding the place where Julie's body had lain. He flopped down into his armchair, sinking at once into what had clearly become an habitual posture, eyes dulled and staring unseeingly at the floor. Thanet and Lineham might not have been in the room for all the awareness he showed of their presence.

Thanet grimaced at Lineham and without a word they cleared a space to sit down on the settee, which was littered with unopened newspapers and half-empty mugs, one of which had overturned, leaving a long brown stain on the golden velvet. Cups and mugs, interspersed with overflowing ashtrays, were scattered everywhere—on the mantelpiece, the floor, the transparent cover of the record-player, in the fireplace, even. There were, however, Thanet noted, no plates. Had Holmes not eaten since Tuesday evening? The air in the room was sour with more than a smell of stale sweat and cigarette smoke; the miasma of despair was so powerful as to be almost tangible.

There was one new feature, though. A painting,

from the face of which the brown paper wrapping had been roughly torn away, stood on the floor, leaning up against one of the legs of the long work table in the bay window. Thanet remembered the flat, oblong parcel which Holmes had almost kicked over in the hall, the last time Thanet came. Shadowed by the table and with its back to the light it was only dimly illuminated, but Thanet thought it looked interesting. It was a painting of a cricket match, on a village green, by the look of it. There was something oddly familiar about the scene and Thanet would have liked to get up and examine it more closely. He refrained from doing so, however—he was not here to appreciate art.

"Mr Holmes?"

Thanet had to repeat the name three times before the dulled eyes swivelled slowly upwards to meet his.

"Mr Holmes, I'm sorry, but I'm afraid there are some more questions I must ask."

No response.

"I know this is painful for you, but it really must be done," Thanet persisted.

Something, the gentleness in his voice, perhaps, provoked a reaction. Holmes's eyes filled with pain and the muscles in his jaw contracted as he clenched his teeth. Then, "It won't bring her back," he said. His voice was rough, either from disuse or from too much smoking.

"No," Thanet said. "But it will, I hope, help us to find out who killed her."

"Yes," said Holmes dully. He made a tiny, helpless gesture with one had. "What the hell," he said. "Who cares?"

"I do," said Thanet.

There was, he now saw, something to be done before he could hope to get anything out of the man. Holmes had sunk into this torpor because it was the least painful way of dealing with an intolerable situation. Somehow, he had to be brought out of it, not only because in this state he was useless to Thanet but for his own sake, because if he went on like this he would surely, eventually, die. There was apparently no one to care whether he lived or not. Perhaps Thanet ought to try to get him into hospital? But he had a horror of interfering in people's lives to such an unwarranted degree, "for their own good." If the man did not wish to go on living, then ultimately the choice was his. Nevertheless, Thanet couldn't just stand by and let it happen.

"Mr Holmes, when did you last have anything to eat?"

"Eat?" A tiny furrow appeared between Holmes's brows, as if he had difficulty in understanding the question.

"Yes, to eat." Thanet gestured at the room. "It looks as though you've been living on coffee."

The frown became more pronounced. "I don't know."

Thanet turned to Lineham. "We won't get anything out of him while he's like this, poor beggar. Go out to the kitchen, see if you can rustle something up, will you? And take some of these mugs with you."

They both got up, collected two fistfuls of mugs each and returned for more. Then Lineham began investigating the contents of the refrigerator and larder while Thanet emptied the ashtrays, finally moving to the bay window and throwing wide open two of the casement windows. Sweet, clean air rushed into the room and Holmes who, during all this activity had remained motionless, turned his head towards the window as if its freshness had touched some chord in his memory.

"Here we are," Lineham said cheerfully, carrying in a tray. "Not very exciting, but the best I can do." The aroma of freshly buttered toast filled the room, a wholesome, appetising smell. Lineham had scrambled some eggs, made a pot of tea.

Holmes ate reluctantly at first and then, his appetite awakened, like a man who had just discovered the existence of food.

Lineham poured cups of tea for Thanet and himself.

"I'll recommend you for the staff canteen," Thanet

said, grinning, as he accepted his. "Now then Mr Holmes, if you're feeling better..."

"Much, thanks." Holmes had lit yet another cigarette, but he was, Thanet thought thankfully, at least looking alive again. The dullness had gone from his eyes, his movements were more positive.

"Good. But before we start, please, try not to let yourself get into that state again."

"Pull myself together, you mean," Holmes said bitterly. "What for?"

"Very well," Thanet said briskly. "It's your choice and I'm not going to argue with you. But for God's sake make it a choice, not an abdication of responsibility. Now, these questions."

Holmes blinked at Thanet's change of tone, but Thanet could see that he had at last given him cause to think. What more could he do? You can't make a man want to live. "Now, I've been to see Mrs Thorpe and there are one or two points I want to clarify. First of all, I understand your wife's father was killed in a road accident. Can you tell me where they were living at the time?"

"London, so far as I know. Julie told me she'd lived in London all her life."

"Which area?"

"Wimbledon, I think. That's where her mother lived, and Julie too, of course, before we got married."

"Your wife had no memories of this crash?"

"No. Not to my knowledge anyway."

"And you've no idea if she was involved in it herself?"

"No. Look here, what's all this about? How can it possibly matter?"

"I've no idea," Thanet said. "I'm trying to understand your wife's state of mind at the time of her death and Mrs Thorpe seemed to think that there might possibly be a connection between this accident and the nightmares your wife had been having lately. Did your wife tell you about them?"

"No, she wouldn't. But they terrified her, all right.

Me too, when she had them. She'd wake up screaming, and the first time it happened . . . It used to take ages to calm her down, afterwards."

"She had them most nights?"

"Every night, since they started."

"Have you any idea why they did start?"

"None at all."

"She'd never had them before?"

"No, never."

"Then something must have triggered them off. Now, I understand that the first one occurred on a Monday evening—that would be a fortnight ago last Monday."

"Something like that, yes."

"Try to think. I must know exactly when they started."

Holmes frowned. "I'm pretty sure—yes, it must have been that Monday, because it was the next day that she rang Mrs Thorpe and that was the day before we were due for an appointment. Yes, it was that Monday."

"Now think very carefully. Can you remember what she did, that day?"

"Not offhand. She must have gone to work, I suppose."

"You can't remember anything special about that Monday?"

Holmes passed a hand over his head and then pressed the thumb and forefinger into his eyes. "I'm sorry. I just can't seem to think . . ."

"Do you think you could try to remember, when we've gone? Try really hard, I mean? And if you do, give me a ring?"

Holmes shrugged. "If you like."

"Good. Now your wife's mother is dead, but if she and your wife lived in the same place all her life until you married, it's possible that your mother-in-law had some close friends living nearby. Do you know of any?"

"There's Mrs Lawton. Julie used to call her Auntie Rose."

"Her address?"

"9 Wellington Road, Wimbledon."

"Any others?"

"Not that I know of."

"Right. There's just one other point." Here it came. Thanet had deliberately left this till last. Now, he kept his tone as casual, as matter-of-fact as possible. "I understand that while you were living in London there was a man who used to pester your wife. Could you give me his name, address and place of work?"

Holmes sat up abruptly. "Kendon, you mean? What's he got to do with it? You don't think he . . . my God, wait till I get my hands on him!"

"Mr Holmes, calm down, please. We really have no idea. But we have to follow up every lead, however slight, and Mrs Thorpe just happened to mention his existence." Thanet felt quite justified in pretending that there was no evidence to connect this man with Julie. For one thing, they were not yet certain that it was he who had apparently been meeting Julie on Tuesday evenings while her husband was out, and for another he didn't want a second murder on his hands; at the moment Holmes looked quite capable of committing one. "Please," he went on. "There really is no need to get so worked up."

"No? If I thought he'd followed her down here . . . He never left her alone, even after we were married. Said she was his, by right—he introduced us, as a matter of fact. He knew her first, but that gave him no rights over her. I told him, it was her choice and that was that. And she chose me." An expression of pride flitted briefly over Holmes's face.

"Anyway, as I said, it's just a matter of checking every lead. So if you could tell us where to find him . . . ?"

"Flat 4, Wallington Park Road, Putney."

"And he worked?"

"At the BBC. He's Kenny Kendon, the disc jockey."

Thanet was astonished, though he didn't show it. Kenny Kendon was one of the Radio 2 regular disc jockeys, with his own live programme each morning. "Description?"

"A bit taller than me—five ten or eleven, I suppose. Brown hair."

So, still in the running for the mysterious boyfriend, Thanet thought with satisfaction. He avoided looking at Lineham. "Well, I think that's about all for the moment." He stood up and Lineham followed suit. "And if you take my advice, Mr Holmes, you'll get back to work as soon as possible. You won't do yourself any good hanging about here, brooding." At the door he turned. "Mrs Thorpe was very concerned about you, by the way. She said she'd give you a ring."

This, he was pleased to see, meant something to Holmes. A spark of interest flared briefly in his eyes. He said nothing, however, as he let them out and watched them walk down the garden path.

"Well, what do you think of that, sir?" Lineham said excitedly, when they were in the car. "Kenny Kendon!"

"Interesting."

"You'll go and see him?"

"Tomorrow, I think. We'll both go, by car. You can visit this Auntie Rose while I'm seeing Kendon."

"Where now, then?" Lineham asked.

Thanet looked at his watch. Four o'clock. "Back to the office. I must get my reports up to date. I'm seeing the Super at five-thirty." At least there were now some interesting developments to report. "Remind me to ring the Met., will you? I'll have to let them know I'll be trespassing on their patch tomorrow."

Nothing interesting awaited them at the office. Thanet managed to bring himself up to date on his paperwork, had a satisfactory interview with superintendent Parker, then took himself home.

The children were already in bed but Bridget heard him arrive and came downstairs, begging for a story. Thanet obliged and then, protesting, did his stint on the rolling-pin while Joan was putting the finishing touches to supper.

"Sylvia rang up," she announced, when they were seated at the table.

Sylvia was an old school friend of Joan's who lived in Borden, a village some ten miles from Sturrenden. "Said she hadn't seen us for far too long, and could we come to dinner on the fifteenth."

"When's that?"

"End of next week."

Thanet grimaced. "It's so tricky."

"I know, and so does she. But it is difficult, with dinner, letting people down at the last minute if you can't make it. Perhaps we'd better say no."

Thanet smiled at her. "Why don't you accept and then, if I can't come at the last minute, go by yourself?"

Joan frowned. "I'd rather go with you."

"I know, but it's hard on you, never having any social life because of my job. Why don't you? You know Sylvia well enough to turn up by yourself if you have to."

"I suppose so," Joan said reluctantly. "All right, I will. I'll say we'll both come if we can, if not I'll come alone."

They ate in companionable silence for a while and then Joan said, "How's the case going?"

Thanet told her. He'd seen so many policemen's marriages fall apart because their wives had been unable to cope with the irregular hours, the inconveniences, the broken promises, the loneliness and sense of isolation, that he had from the beginning vowed that this would never happen to him. He believed that if a wife felt involved in her husband's work she could more easily tolerate the demands it made upon her. Many of his colleagues, he knew, would disagree, would say that the only way to cope with pressures that were often near-intolerable was to keep their working and home lives completely separate, shut the former out of their minds the moment they stepped through the front door.

But for Thanet and Joan his way had worked, kept them close to each other. He trusted her completely, knew that she would never betray a confidence. What was more, talking to her often served to clarify his thoughts.

"Kenny Kendon!" she said, echoing Lineham, when he had finished. "You're going to see him?"

"Tomorrow."

"That'll be interesting. Seeing the inside of Broadcasting House and so on." She laughed at his expression. "All right, I know that's not what you're going for. All the same, it *will* be interesting. Out of the usual run."

"True." He could see that that was how it might seem to her. Her life at the moment was very much dictated by the demands of domesticity, above all by the needs of the children. And, as anyone knows who has experienced it, the unremitting company of small children can be very wearing, however much one loves them. He leaned across, took her hand. "Do you get very fed up with these four walls, love?"

She grimaced. "Sometimes, I suppose, if I'm honest. But I tell myself it won't go on for ever. I'm glad you're not one of those Victorian types, though, who'd like to see his wife shut up in them for good. And you can stop looking so smug!"

Thanet grinned. "Me, look smug? Nonsense!"

"All the same, it's nice to get some vicarious glimpse of the outside world, especially if there's a spot of glamour involved. Promise you'll be especially observant, tomorrow."

"Cross my heart," Thanet said.

7

Thanet and Lineham set off for London at half past seven the next morning. Thanet had checked the times of Kendon's daily programme in the Radio Times: seven-thirty to ten o'clock. He hoped to arrive at Broadcasting House in comfortable time to catch Kendon when the programme ended.

On the way they tuned in to Radio 2 and listened with interest to Kendon's show, which proved to be the usual mixture of chat, jokes, phone-ins, record requests and pop music. It was comforting to know that their quarry was certain to be there, at the end of the trail. After a while Thanet switched off and they drove in silence.

"You know what strikes me as odd about this case, sir?" Lineham said eventually.

"What?" Thanet took out his pipe and started to fill it.

"The number of men who were interested in Mrs Holmes. I mean, the one thing that's obvious is that she was attractive to men. There's her husband, who was potty about her, Mr Parrish—according to Miss Waters, anyway—and now this man Kendon."

"What's so strange about that? Some women are especially attractive to men." Thanet lit up and waved his hands to disperse the clouds of smoke billowing around them.

"Yes, but this girl was different, wasn't she? I

mean, often, when you get a woman who attracts men, it's because she's, well . . ."

"Sexy?" supplied Thanet with a mischievous grin. He never quite understood how Lineham had managed thus far to preserve a certain naivety in such matters. One would have imagined he'd have shed that long ago, in this job.

"Yes." Lineham kept his eyes studiously on the road. "And this girl wasn't . . . sexy, or at least, if she was she didn't seem conscious of it—even Miss Waters, who admits to being jealous of her, says that."

"I know. But, for a start, I don't agree that girls who are attractive to men are necessarily sexy, even if they appear to be so. There's a certain type of girl, for instance, who is so unsure of her attractiveness—her femininity if you like—that she deliberately sets out to attract men, to appear sexy, to prove something to herself. Women like that are often cold underneath, frigid even, and frequently end up with the reputation of being heartless flirts. But Julie Holmes, I'm pretty sure, didn't fall into this category. As you say, even Maureen Waters, who admits to being jealous of her, says that Julie seemed unaware of her effect on men and certainly didn't set out deliberately to impress them.

"Anyway, the point is that because of the sort of person she was, Julie was under constant pressure from the men in her life, each of whom seems to have seen her as a unique challenge and was therefore not prepared to give up easily. Somehow, by her very nature, she invited it."

"You mean she was a natural victim, sir?"

"In a way, yes, I suppose I do. But I think it was a little more complicated than that. I think that under normal circumstances she could cope with pressure of the kind we've been talking about. The trouble started when something extra came along."

"The nightmares, you mean?"

"It looks like it, from what we've been told."

"But why should they have made that much differ-

ence? I mean, people often have nightmares, but they
don't go to pieces because of them."

"I don't think that these were just ordinary
nightmares." Thanet was gazing out of the window. They
were now entering the outer suburbs and part of his
mind was automatically mourning the rape of the
countryside. "They frightened her, of course, exhausted
her probably because they disturbed her sleep, but I
would guess they started because something deep in
her mind had been stirred up, something that was best
forgotten."

"What sort of thing, sir?"

"Who knows? But," Thanet said dreamily, still
gazing at the monotonous pattern of houses, "I would
guess that it was something very nasty indeed. A verita-
ble Kraken."

"A what, sir?"

Thanet shot him an amused glance. "A monster,
Mike. A sleeping sea-monster which, suddenly awakened,
stirs up an awful lot of mud. So that's one of the things I
want you to do when talking to this Mrs Lawton, Julie's
Auntie Rose. Keep an eye out for monsters."

"You mean, try to find out if Mrs Holmes had any
traumatic experiences as a child, sir?"

"Oh, for God's sake, man, stop being so pompous.
But yes, that's exactly what I do mean."

"Sir . . . ?"

"Yes?"

"No, it doesn't matter."

Thanet suppressed his irritation and said softly,
"Look Mike, let me just tell you this. It's as good a time
as any. I may be a bit impatient with you at times, but
the only thing that really irritates me about you is your
lack of self-confidence. It's such a waste, you see. The
powers that be have had the wisdom to see that it
doesn't stop you from being a first-rate copper, and no
doubt hoped that early promotion would give your ego
a boost. So give yourself a chance, will you? If you have
a suggestion to make, make it."

"It's not so much an idea as a question." Lineham

shot a quick, assessing glance at Thanet. "It's just that I can't see the point of digging into the girl's past. What does it matter to us, if she saw something nasty in the woodshed at the age of three?"

Now that Lineham had actually spoken out and had criticised him, Thanet irrationally felt angry—and then, almost at once, amused at himself. Typical, he thought. Encourage the man to express his ideas, then get mad because they're not the same as yours. "I can quite see your point," he said. "But I can't agree with you, not at the moment. I have a feeling that her state of mind at the time was directly responsible for her death, and that it is therefore very important to know what was disturbing her. Anyway, until we actually have the murderer in our hands my policy is always to dig and go on digging, irrespective of what turns up."

"I will duly dig," said Lineham solemnly, then flashed a wicked, sideways glance at Thanet to see how he had taken the remark.

Thanet grinned and gave the sergeant a playful slap on the shoulder before turning to study his map. The traffic was thickening now and Lineham had to give his full attention to his driving. Thanet directed him. They crossed Blackfriars Bridge, found their way into the Strand, circled around Trafalgar Square, drove up to Piccadilly Circus. Thanet experienced the familiar surge of excitement which London always induced in him. The knowledge that he was at the hub of one of the greatest cities in the world never failed to affect him. They battled their way along Regent Street, negotiated Oxford Circus and experienced a sense of triumph as the greyish-white bulk of Broadcasting House loomed up ahead of them, dwarfing the delicate spire, slender columns and satisfying symmetry of All Souls Church. It was twenty to ten.

"Pick me up here at eleven-thirty," Thanet said. "You're sure you'll find your way?"

Lineham nodded. "I took a good look at the maps last night."

"Fine. See you then."

Thanet watched Lineham out of sight around the one-way system, then turned to look up at the solid mass of Broadcasting House. Above the tall, golden doors was an impressive sculpture of an old man holding a young child. Thanet studied it for a moment, wondering what it symbolised, before going into the foyer. He crossed to the reception desk on his right and said that he wished to speak urgently to Mr Kendon. Deliberately he did not reveal that he was a policeman; he did not want to put Kendon on his guard.

The receptionist told him what he already knew, that Kendon was busy at the moment with his programme. She said that she would ring up to leave the message that someone was waiting to see him, and assured Thanet that Kendon would come down as soon as he was free. Thanet thanked her and sat down to wait on one of the red benches in the reception area, looking about him with interest.

The foyer was alive with movement. A constant stream of people flowed past the two security men behind the rope barrier. These, he noticed, were meticulously careful; during the next twenty minutes nobody entered the inner area without showing his pass. Remembering his promise to Joan, Thanet kept his eyes open for familiar faces but, disappointingly, there were none. Scarcely surprising, he reflected. If this had been the television centre, now . . .

It seemed no time at all before Kendon presented himself.

"Mr Thanet?"

Thanet rose as he acknowledged the greeting, studying Kendon with interest. The barmaid's description had been very accurate, he thought, and he could see why Kendon had made such an impression on her. Like Parrish, this man would be very attractive to women. He had rugged good looks, a find physique, and considerable charm. He was wearing a white silk polo-necked shirt and tight dark green trousers in a fine, silky corduroy velvet. He looked disconcerted when Thanet produced his identification card, but soon appeared to recover his aplomb.

"We'll go across to the Langham," he said. "We'll be able to talk quietly there."

As they pushed their way out through the tall swing doors and crossed the road, Kendon kept up a smooth monologue. They were, he said, going to the Club, a favourite haunt of those who worked for the BBC. The Langham used to be the Langham Hotel, and had been taken over by the BBC, famous ghost and all. Thanet stored it all up to tell Joan, wondering if this was Kendon's normal way of carrying on a conversation (if such it could be called) or whether the man was simply talking in order to forestall questions before he was ready to answer them.

More tall golden doors, green carpet, left along corridors to a high, spacious room furnished with small round tables, a bar on one side and a buffet on the other. Kendon insisted on paying for the coffee before leading the way to the far end of the room where a huge bay window overlooked the busy street below.

"It's just been redecorated," Kendon said, looking about with a proprietorial air.

"Very nice," Thanet said obediently. "And now, Mr Kendon..."

"Of course, of course," Kendon said hurriedly. He sipped his coffee, set the cup down and sat back with an air of compliant readiness. "How can I help you, Inspector?"

"I believe you knew Julie Holmes," Thanet said. He caught the flash of real pain in Kendon's eyes before the man's features assembled themselves into an appropriate expression of solemnity.

"Yes, I did know her once, quite well, as a matter of fact. I read about her . . . her death in the papers, of course." He sipped at his coffee again. "A terrible business."

Thanet merely nodded, saying nothing. He frequently found silence a more effective weapon than questions. Few people could tolerate it for long. Kendon proved no exception. He took a further sip of coffee, put his cup down and looked uneasily at Thanet. Then he took out a cigarette case, offered it to the inspector and, when he refused, took a cigarette himself and lit up.

Thanet continued to sip his coffee and wait. ·

Kendon became increasingly uncomfortable as the silence stretched out between them, puffing at his cigarette with jerky, uneven movements and fidgeting on his chair. At last he could stand it no longer.

"Well?" he demanded.

"Well what?" Thanet said blandly.

Kendon gesticulated with his cigarette, scattering ash into his coffee. He swore. "What did you want to see me about?"

"I'm just waiting for you to tell me about Julie Holmes."

"What d'you mean, tell you about her? Look here, Inspector, if you think I had anything to do with her murder..."

"Did I say that?" Thanet said mildly. "Just tell me about her. About your relationship with her." He was satisfied, now, that Kendon was sufficiently on the defensive to be vulnerable. It seemed, however, that he had underestimated his man.

Kendon leaned forward. "OK Inspector, I'll level with you. There's no point in doing anything else, I suppose. She was a drag. Wouldn't leave me alone. Even after she was married, even after she moved down to Kent."

Thanet hid his astonishment at this unexpectedly mirror-image version of the relationship between Kendon and Julie as he had envisaged it. "Go on," he said.

Kendon stubbed out his cigarette. "I thought I'd finally shaken her off when she married John—I introduced them, you know. I was always introducing her to men I hoped might get her off my back. And this time it seemed to work—for a while. For a couple of months I heard nothing from her and then it all started again. Letters, phone-calls... it drove me mad. But I felt sorry for her, in a way, and I used to meet her from time to time, to keep her happy."

"Even to the extent of going down to Kent once a week to see her?"

"Sure, why not?"

"Why, Mr Kendon?"

Kendon shrugged. "I told you. I felt sorry for her. I had a soft spot for her. There was something, well, a bit pathetic about her. I was always afraid she might, well, you know, do something drastic."

"Commit suicide, you mean?"

"Yeah."

"If you didn't see her?"

"Right. Look Inspector, my job has, well, a certain glamour about it. Girls like that, they go for it. Julie was no different from any of the others."

"And you put yourself out for all these lovesick maidens to the extent of sacrificing one evening a week to keep them happy?"

"Of course not. But I told you, I had a soft spot for Julie."

"Go on."

"With what?"

"Well, let's take last Tuesday for a start, shall we? The night she died."

"Yeah, well," Kendon ran his tongue over his lower lip, "that was all a bit . . . I suppose the people in the pub remembered us?"

"They did."

"Not surprising, the way she took off. It was like this. I'd decided this was the last time I was trailing all the way down there to see her and told her so. She didn't like it, she begged, pleaded with me, but I told her I'd finally had enough and that was that. In the end she got very upset and ran off."

None of this fitted in with the way the barmaid had described the quarrel but Thanet was ready to let this pass. It was the next bit that really interested him. "Go on."

Kendon leaned back in his chair, lifted his hands in a gesture of finality.

"That's it."

Thanet looked at him in silence for a moment, considering which line would be most likely to produce the truth. Kendon's story was obviously going to be that after the quarrel he made his way back to the station and caught a train back to London. The question was, if he were allowed to produce this story, how would he react to being accused of lying? Would he cave in, or would he dig his heels in? Probably the latter, Thanet thought. Kendon's opinion of himself was such that he would always find it difficult to climb down. It would be better to make sure that the man did not find himself in that position.

"Not quite, I think, Mr Kendon. I must be frank and tell you that not only were you seen to follow Mrs Holmes when you left the pub, but that two independent witnesses saw you very close to Gladstone Road around twenty to nine."

The man was cool, Thanet thought, watching him. He did not so much as blink, but merely gave a little shrug of submission, a wry grin.

"Ah well, it was worth a try... All right, Inspector, I'll tell you the rest of it. As I said, I was absolutely fed up with the situation. I wanted Julie to understand that I had really meant what I said, that I didn't want her pestering me any more and that this was the last time I'd trail all the way down to Kent to calm her down. The way she left... well, nothing had been resolved. She'd just run away from the situation, refused to face up to it and I could see it all going on exactly as it had before. So I finished my drink, gave her a few minutes to cool down, then followed her. Well, I say I followed her, but in fact she was out of sight all the way. There are a lot of turnings, in a very short distance, between that pub and where she lived. But I was sure she'd have gone home, so when I got to Gladstone Road I just marched up the path and knocked on the front door. She came to the bay window in the front room to see who it was—I just caught a glimpse of her before she disappeared. Anyway, she didn't come to the door straight away, so I knocked again."

For the first time, now, Kendon's composure showed signs of slipping. "I heard her steps in the hall and thought she was coming to let me in, but suddenly she shouted—well, screamed, really,—'Look through the letter box, Kenny.' So I did." Kendon leaned forward and his eyes flickered from side to side as if he were making sure that there was nobody within earshot, then he said softly, intensely, "She was standing there holding a bloody great carving knife, Inspector! 'Go away!' she was screaming, 'Go away, or I'll stick this in you!' And she shook the thing at me!"

Kendon leaned sideways to extract a handkerchief from his trouser pocket and mopped at the sheen of perspiration on his forehead.

"And then?" said Thanet.

Kendon hesitated, ran his tongue over his lips. Clearly, he realised that this was the crucial point. Then he shrugged, leaned back, seemed to relax a little, as if he'd decided how to handle it. "Oh come on, Inspector. Put yourself in my position. I'd played along with her for years, trailed down to Kent to see her regularly. It was a drag, I can tell you. And what happens when I finally decide I've got to make the break? She threatens me with a bloody great knife, for God's sake! When I saw her standing there like that I thought, that's it. I've bloody well had enough."

"You were angry," Thanet said softly.

"I bloody well was!" Kendon suddenly realised what he was saying and leaned forward earnestly in his chair. "Oh, don't get me wrong, Inspector. I wasn't angry enough to kill her. Why should I risk my neck for her? No, like I said, I just thought she could go to hell as far as I was concerned. So I just walked away. I'd only got as far as the gate when I heard the front door open behind me. She was still waving the knife. 'Don't ever come back,' she was screaming. And, believe me, I didn't intend to."

"So what did you do then?"

"Went to the station and caught a train home."

"Which train did you catch?"

"The eight fifty-four."

And Manson had said that it took six minutes to walk to the station from Holmes's house.

"Did you have to wait long, on the station?"

"Only a minute or two."

Thanet was silent for a moment, thinking over what he had heard. "Is there anyone who can corroborate what you have told me?"

The answer was a surprise. "As a matter of fact, yes." Kendon lit a fresh cigarette and inhaled deeply before going on. His self-possession had returned and there was even a hint of malicious satisfaction in his eyes. "When Julie opened the front door and shouted at me I started off down the road towards the footpath, and there was this girl ahead of me, near the swing gate. I think she must have come along the footpath beside the wire fence, the one that links the ends of all those cul-de-sacs. Anyway, she obviously heard Julie because she stopped and glanced up the road towards us. Then she went on, through the swing gate and along the footpath. I caught her up and passed her just before we reached the station. She caught the same train as me. So you see, Inspector, I'm in the clear. Find that girl and she'll tell you that Julie was alive when I left her, and that I had no chance to slip back and kill her afterwards."

"I see. Could you give us a description of this girl, to help us trace her?"

Kendon leanded back in his chair, narrowed his eyes in recollection. "Mid-twenties, I should think. I'm afraid I didn't really notice her face, so she must have been pretty nondescript. After all, I didn't know I was going to need her, did I, or I'd have taken down her name and address, so to speak! Hair dark, I think. Yes, dark, straight, shoulder-length."

"How tall?"

"Oh, medium. About five five, I should think."

"What was she wearing?"

Kendon frowned in concentration. "Nothing very striking, that's for sure. Something dark—yes, a dark coat, brown, I think. She was just an ordinary sort of girl."

"Unfortunately."

"Unfor . . . oh, yes, I see." Kendon looked anxious. "You think she'll be difficult to trace?"

Thanet shrugged. "Who knows? We'll have to wait and see."

"And hope," Kendon said drily.

"Yes, and hope. Did anyone else catch that train, by the way?"

"There were one or two other people on the platform, yes. But I honestly can't remember anything about them. To be frank, I was still very upset, after the scene with Julie. I kept on remembering how she looked, through that letter box. . . . Honestly, Inspector, she looked demented. Really demented. I couldn't seem to think of much else all the way back on the train . . . Do you think I shouldn't have left her in that state?" he asked abruptly.

So the man was feeling guilty, asking for reassurance, Thanet thought. As well he might be. For his, after all, had been the hand which had given Julie the final push that sent her over the edge. On the other hand he had not been responsible for the forces which had gathered to drive her there. "In a situation like that it's difficult to know what should be done for the best," he said non-committally.

"Oh come on, Inspector," Kendon burst out. "What would you have done, tell me that?"

It was a cry from the heart and for the first time Thanet felt a twinge of genuine compassion for Kendon. Faced with the man and his smooth recital of the story Thanet had almost forgotten that if what he had previously learnt were true, Kendon had been in love with Julie for years. Now he had dropped his defences. Whatever Thanet thought of the man it would be inhuman to

refuse to take his question seriously. "I don't know," he
said. "Called a doctor, perhaps?"

Kendon sat back. "I feel so bloody guilty about it.
If only I hadn't just left her like that, perhaps she'd still
be alive... There's something I haven't told you," he
added abruptly. "I'm still not sure about it, you see. If I
had been, I'd have contacted you before now, myself."

So it could be important, Thanet thought. He
made an encouraging noise. Kendon hesitated a moment longer before saying, "It's just that when I reached
the swing gate I turned back to glance at the house, see
if Julie was still there." He stopped.

"And was she?"

"No, but in the instant when I turned away again, I
had the impression of movement, at the corner of the
street..."

Thanet experienced a sudden lurch of excitement
in the pit of his stomach. It was as if he had just
glimpsed the murderer, out of the corner of his eye. "At
the far end of Gladstone Road, you mean?"

"Yes. It was just an impression, as I say, but
looking back I'm pretty certain that someone was just
turning into Gladstone Road."

"A man or a woman?"

Kendon shook his head. "It's no use. I've thought
and thought and I still don't know. It really was no more
than a flicker of movement on the very edge of my
vision, before I turned away."

"Well if you do remember, give me a ring at once,
will you?" Thanet scribbled both his home and office
numbers on a piece of paper, handed it over and stood
up. "I think that's about all for the moment, Mr Kendon."

Kendon followed suit. "I'm sorry I couldn't have
been more helpful."

He seemed to mean it and Thanet found that the
last few minutes of their conversation had somewhat
altered his feelings towards the man. They chatted
amiably enough as they made their way back out on to
the street. Kendon turned right and made his way off
down Regent Street. Hands in pockets and head down,

he looked thoroughly despondent. An act? Thanet
wondered, as he watched him out of sight. He rather
thought not.

"You think he was telling the truth?" Lineham asked
when they had negotiated their way through the worst
of the traffic and Thanet had given him an account of
the interview.

"In his version of his relationship with Julie, no, I
don't. It just doesn't fit in with what her husband and
Mrs Thorpe told us. Or with the barmaid's account of
their quarrel, for that matter. And I would say he just
isn't the type to put himself out to that degree for a
former girlfriend. No, I would guess he was just saving
face, making it sound as if she was the one who was
doing the chasing. But in the important thing, in his
account of what actually happened on Tuesday night,
then yes, I think perhaps I do. I'm inclined to, anyway.
We'll have to do some checking—see if we can trace
that girl he claims to have followed to the station. We'll
put out an appeal, see what turns up. Or perhaps the
ticket collector will be able to help us. If there weren't
many people on that train it's just possible he might
have some recollection of her. Kendon might have
invented her, of course, and the same could be said of
this mysterious person he claims to have seen turning
into Gladstone Road. But if there really was somebody..."

"It could be our murderer."

"It's possible. I think we'd better go over all those
house-to-house reports again and re-question everybody
who was not stuck in front of *The Pacemakers*. What
about you? How did you get on with Mrs Lawton?"

"Fine. I think I got everything we needed."

Julie and her mother had apparently moved to
London from Kent when Julie was three, after her
father's accident, buying a small terraced hourse in one
of the respectable but less wealthy areas of Wimbledon.
Julie had lived there until her marriage, her mother
until her death a year ago.

For some time after the move from Kent Julie had
suffered from nightmares but Mrs Lawton had no idea

of their content and had at the time thought of them as normal under the circumstances, Julie having lost her father so suddenly. Julie had not been involved in the accident that killed him, Mrs Lawton had been positive about that, and Julie's mother had told her friend that she had moved because she wanted to get right away from the place which had so many associations with her husband. She had never remarried.

"Where did they live in Kent?" Thanet asked, when Lineham had finished.

"Little Sutton."

"Little Sutton," Thanet repeated slowly. He knew the village, of course, it wasn't far from where Sylvia, Joan's friend, lived. But in this particular context it struck some kind of chord. What was it? He frowned out of the window, trying to put his finger on it. He couldn't, and after a while he gave up. The feeling remained, however, and all the way home it remained lodged at the back of his mind, as uncomfortable as a grain of sand under an eyelid.

As soon as they got back to the office, Thanet sent for the file on the accident in which Julie's father had been killed while Lineham drafted the appeal for the witness Kendon claimed could clear him. It was still only half past two and with any luck they should catch the evening editions of the national newspapers.

They then worked together through the house-to-house reports, deciding which people should be interviewed again. At Lineham's suggestion one man would be detailed to knock on every door in the three streets with instructions to find out the names of all women between the ages of fifteen and thirty-five living there and their movements on the night of the murder. It was possible, of course, that the woman Kendon claimed to have seen came from quite another area but, as Lineham pointed out, only someone with local knowledge would have known about that footpath. It was worth checking.

By now the file had arrived and while Lineham went off to make arrangements Thanet settled down to study it. He wasn't quite sure why he was doing this; on

the face of it, the accident could have no relevance to
the present enquiry. He simply felt that he should and
experience had taught him that such feelings should be
indulged. They were frequently based on connections
made by his subconscious, connections which seemed
obvious on looking back but which at the time seemed
irrational or non-existent.

David Leonard Parr of Jasmine Cottage, The Green,
Little Sutton, Kent, had died on November 18, 1960 in
Sturrenden General Hospital at eight pm, five hours
after his car had been in collision with a lorry in dense
fog on the main Sturrenden to Maidstone road. The
lorry driver had been unhurt and had later been cleared
of any responsibility for the crash; Parr had been on the
wrong side of the road and had skidded after going too
fast into a bend which he had presumably been unable
to see because of the fog. He had been twenty-nine
years old and had been alone in the car.

Thanet read all the statements through twice, quickly,
and then more slowly a third time. His instinct, he
decided, had let him down. Try as he would he could
not see that the accident to Julie's father had any
bearing on her murder. Reading the report had been a
waste of time. He closed the file and pushed it away
with a gesture of disgust.

He stood up and moved to the window. Outside,
the streets were crowded with people going home from
work and traffic had come to a standstill at the pelican
crossing a hundred yards or so away up the road to the
left. It had been a mistake to install one on such a busy
road, Thanet thought. A constant stream of people
pressing the crossing control-button could make it virtually
impossible for traffic to keep moving. A conventional
system of traffic lights would have been better, with an
integrated pedestrian crossing control system. He really
must remember to raise the matter with Traffic Control.

He felt as sluggish as the traffic below him. He
hated this stage in a case, when the initial impetus
seems to have slipped away and the possibility of failure
rears its ugly head. Thanet privately thought of this

time as the policeman's Slough of Despond. Not that such thoughts were put into words. On the contrary, there seemed to be a conspiracy of silence on the subject and Thanet sometimes wondered if many men superstitiously refused to acknowledge their doubts even to themselves, lest merely entertaining the possibility of failure should somehow blight their chances of success.

He knew that by now he ought to have had enough experience to be able to tell himself that his depression was normal, something to be expected at this stage of a case, but the trouble was that each time it happened came the fear that this time would be different, this time there would be no breakthrough, that he would have, eventually, to admit defeat.

The thought was enough to make him grit his teeth and turn back to his desk. There was only one way to deal with a mood like this and that was to immerse himself totally in work, to revert to patient, thorough, routine investigation. He must sit down, reread all the reports that had come in on the case so far, check, re-check and cross-check, discuss the matter exhaustively with Lineham and try and see what they had missed, what their next moves ought to be.

He pressed the buzzer on his desk. "Find Lineham for me, will you?"

8

By the time Thanet arrived home at half past eight he felt as though his brain were stuffed with cotton wool. He and Lincham had gone over and over every scrap of information they had so far accumulated, had endlessly discussed the possible guilt of their three main suspects— Holmes, Parrish and Kendon, and had failed completely to reach any satisfactory conclusion or to see any way of breaking out of the impasse they seemed to have reached.

Joan took one look at his face and unobtrusively took charge. Thanet was shepherded into the living-room where Joan told him to sit down and relax, thrust a large drink into his hand and disappeared into the kitchen. Thanet sat gazing into space, sipping his whisky and thinking about absolutely nothing until she reappeared with a tray. He had thought he wasn't hungry but the sight and smell of one of his favourite dishes; steak and kidney pudding, revived his appetite and by the time he laid down his knife and fork he was beginning to feel human again.

Joan, sitting opposite him, watched in companionable silence. "Better?" she said, finally, when he had finished, whisking away the tray.

Thanet stretched his legs out before him, loosened his belt one notch and patted his stomach ostentatiously. "Much," he said.

"Good. I'll fetch the coffee."

Thanet waited, gazing absentmindedly at the painting which hung on the wall before him, above the fireplace. It was an original oil which Joan had found unframed in a junk shop, shortly after they were married. She had managed to unearth an antique dealer who carried a stock of old picture frames, had persuaded him to cut one down to fit and had hung the finished product in pride of place. Thanet had always liked the painting, which was of a rural scene—cows grazing in the water meadows along the banks of a river. Such pictures, although not especially valuable had become increasingly difficult to find, Joan said. She'd always been interested in Art and lately had been talking about taking a three-year course in the History of Painting at the College of Art when Ben was old enough to go to school.

"I forgot to tell you," Thanet said when she returned with the coffee, "I saw an interesting picture yesterday."

"What was it? A portrait?"

"Landscape, I suppose. It was of a cricket match, on a village green. Very vivid colours and lots of tiny figures."

"Really? It sounds like a Dacre. She specialised in village scenes. *Village Wedding, Church Fête, Shrove Tuesday*—that one was of a pancake race—and so on. As a matter of fact, I'm sure I remember the one you're talking about." She rose, started rummaging through a pile of papers and leaflets on a low table in the angle of the chimney breast. "I've got a catalogue here, somewhere. The style sounds typically hers, as I said—lots of tiny figures, brilliant colours. Ah," she said triumphantly. "Here it is."

She sat down beside Thanet, opened the catalogue and ran her finger down the list of exhibits. "Yes, I thought so. Here we are. *The Cricket Match*. By courtesy of..." her voice slowed, wavered before going on, "Mrs Julie Holmes."

"Let me see!" Thanet stared at the entry, his mind racing. The painting, then, had obviously just been returned from the exhibition—he remembered seeing the package in Holmes's hall on... which day had it been?

The day before yesterday? Yes, that was right. Wednesday, then.

"When did you go to this exhibition, darling?"

"On Tuesday."

Surely it would have taken longer than that to dismantle the exhibits? Apparently not. Here was the evidence, in print, before him. A thought occurred to him. When had the exhibition started? He looked at the front page of the catalogue. It had been, apparently, a memorial exhibition to mark the twentieth anniversary of the death of Annabel Dacre, and had been open to the public from Tuesday, April 22 to May 6. The Private View had been held on the evening of Monday, April 21.

Thanet sat up with a jerk. "Who would have attended the Private View?"

Joan shrugged. "Local big-wigs, I suppose. Local artists, probably. And, of course, all the people who had loaned the paintings."

Julie had loaned a painting. And on Monday, April 21 she had had that nightmare for the first time.

Thanet went to the telephone and rang Holmes. It sounded as though Holmes had pulled himself together for he was unusually forthcoming. He had forgotten about it but yes, now that Thanet mentioned it, he and Julie had both attended the Private View. They had received an invitation because Julie had loaned a painting. Holmes had found the occasion very boring. They knew nobody, and he wasn't interested in art anyway. Julie had wanted to go because she liked the idea of the privilege of attending a private view and because she'd thought it might be a chance to meet a few more local people. No, nothing unusual had happened during the evening. Julie had been rather quiet on the way home, but he'd thought that was because she'd been a little disappointed that they hadn't enjoyed themselves as much as she had hoped. The painting had belonged to Julie's mother. Julie had found it tucked away in a box in the attic when she was clearing out the house in Wimbledon after her mother's death. Then, when she'd seen the advertisement in the *Sturrenden Gazette*, she was rather tickled at the idea of lending the picture and having "By courtesy of Mrs Julie Holmes" in the catalogue. The advertisement had announced that a memorial exhibition of Annabel Dacre's work was to be arranged and requested the loan of examples of her work.

Thanet went back into the living-room, sat down and began to read the biography on the back of the catalogue. The first line brought him up short and he experienced that unique elation that comes when one suddenly understands something which has been puzzling one, that sudden fusing of apparently unrelated facts into a coherent whole so obvious that one wonders why on earth one hasn't seen it before.

"Darling, what on earth's the matter?" Joan had just come in with fresh coffee.

"Annabel Dacre was born and brought up in Little Sutton!"

"Yes, I know. What of it?"

Thanet jumped up, wincing as his back protested, and began to pace up and down. "Well it's just that there have been one or two things nagging away at the back of my mind, and I couldn't work out why. I knew, when I found out that the Parrs—Julie Holmes's parents—had lived in Little Sutton, that there was some reason why the name rang a bell—apart from the fact that I knew the place, that is. I'd seen that painting at Holmes's house, you see, and knew that there was something familiar about it. It was the background of course, the village green at Little Sutton. You know those two huge oaks, slightly off centre . . . Why on earth didn't I see it before?"

"Darling, do stop pacing about like that. You're making me dizzy. Sit down, and explain why you're so excited about it."

Thanet subsided on to the settee. "Look. As a child Julie—Julie Parr, as she then was, lived in Little Sutton. We found that out today. And it was in Little Sutton, presumably, that one of her parents bought the picture of the cricket match. Now when Julie is three her father is killed in a car crash and at once Mrs Parr, anxious to get away from painful memories, leaves the village and moves to London. She can't bring herself to destroy the picture—perhaps it had been a gift from her husband, but neither can she bear to look at it. So she tucks it away in the attic and for twenty years no one but she knows of its existence.

"Julie grows up, gets married, her mother dies and Julie finds the picture when clearing out the house. Then her husband's firm transfers him to Sturrenden. She moves with him, having no idea that she once lived in Kent, her mother for some reason having given her to understand they'd always lived in London. She is intrigued to read in the local paper that Sturrenden College of Art is appealing for the loan of paintings by Annabel Dacre for a special memorial exhibition. She offers to lend hers, is invited to the Private View, attends it with her husband—and that night she has the first in a series of nightmares which frighten her to such a degree that she asks her counsellor for a private interview and is sick after telling her about them. Even the people at work notice that she is looking ill—jumpy, nervous, was how one girl described it."

"So you think something happened at that Private view to . . . to what?"

"To, how shall I put it, reactivate something which had had a profound effect on Julie as a child."

"But even if that is true, how can it possibly be relevant to her murder?"

"I don't know." Thanet struck one clenched fist into the palm of the other. "I just don't know. I just have this feeling . . ." Thanet picked up the catalogue again and quickly read the rest of the biographical details on the back. "What does it mean, 'tragic early death'?"

"I've no idea. As it says, Annabel Dacre was only twenty-five when she died. And it *was* tragic. I think the world lost a fine painter."

"And that was twenty years ago. 1960. The same year Mrs Parr moved to London."

"But that was because her husband was killed."

"Yes, but it's a coincidence, and although coincidences do happen, I like to make sure that's what they really are." Thanet tossed the catalogue on the table, turned to Joan, put his arm around her. "I think a little visit to the College of Art is indicated, in the morning."

Joan grinned. "It's Saturday tomorrow."

"Damn. So it is. Never mind, I expect we'll be able to dig someone up."

He didn't doubt it. His mood of despondency had melted away and he felt buoyant, confident, on course again. He certainly wasn't going to be defeated by red tape.

He almost was, however. It took over an hour of telephone calls to get around the fact that the entire educational system of Kent closed down on Saturdays. In the end it was Lineham who, through a friend of a friend who was a student at the College of Art, managed to get hold of the man who was Head of Fine Arts at the College, and that only after working systematically through all the Johnsons in the local directory.

"At last," Lineham said, triumphant but weary, handing the telephone over to Thanet.

Mr Johnson was not very pleased at having his weekend plans interrupted, but agreed, reluctantly, to see Inspector Thanet.

"I'll be there in twenty minutes," said Thanet. "Thank you, sir."

The Johnsons lived on a small, pleasant estate of individually designed modern houses which had been built in the grounds of a large country house in a village two miles out of Sturrenden. Each stood in a beautifully landscaped plot of about half an acre, generously endowed with mature trees which were obviously a legacy from the original gardens of the stately home. Thanet wondered how on earth the builders had managed to get planning permission. "Infilling"? he wondered.

From the outside the Johnsons' house was pleasant but unremarkable: large windows, random stonework, pleasantly mellow red brick. Inside, however, it was a very different kettle of fish. Only half the house had a first floor, the other half being one huge room open right up to the exposed roof rafters. It was divided into several clearly defined areas: a studio area with tall windows on the north side, an eating area and, fascinatingly, a sitting area which consisted of a kind of pit sunk into the floor, its edges defined by thickly padded bench seats, the whole close-carpeted in velvety peacock blue. Joan would have loved to see this, Thanet thought.

Johnson led the way down the three steps which descended into the pit and waved Thanet on to one of the benches. He was tall, stooping, half bald, with a tiny, wispy beard, sunken eyes and surprisingly luxuriant eyebrows. Thanet had clearly interrupted his work. He was wearing a paint-stained smock and scuffed moccasins.

"I must apologise for my reluctance on the telephone, Inspector," he said with a rueful smile, "but I'm afraid my free time is very limited and I always try to devote Saturdays to painting. I should have realised, however, that crime doesn't take the weekend off, so I hope you will forgive me."

A girl of about seventeen, long-haired and barefoot, had silently approached with a tray. Thanet smiled his thanks as he accepted the coffee. The mug was of a striking design, pot-bellied and out-curving at the rim and thrown in satisfying heavy rough-surfaced stoneware.

"The work of one of our most promising young potters, a boy called Denzil Runyon," Johnson said, noting Thanet's interest.

"Very attractive indeed," Thanet said. "No, I'm the one who should be apologising, Mr Johnson, for disturbing you at your work. But as you say, crime isn't a Monday-to-Friday business."

"So how can I help?"

"I'd be grateful if you would tell me about the Dacre Exhibition—who suggested it, how it was set up and so on. I'm afraid I'm not at liberty to explain my interest, and indeed the information might prove to be

irrelevant to the enquiry upon which I'm working. But
we must follow up every lead, you understand."

"So my curiosity will remain unsatisfied. What a
pity. Well, never mind. I must grin and bear it, mustn't
I? Yes, well now, let me see. The Exhibition was
suggested by Annabel Dacre's mother."

Thanet was startled. He hadn't thought that Mrs
Dacre would still be alive, but now, of course, he
realised that it was quite feasible that she should be. If
Annabel Dacre had been only twenty-five when she
died, twenty years ago, and her mother had been, say,
between forty-five and fifty-five at the time . . .

"She's in her early seventies now, and very frail.
I've known her for many years and have long been
aware of her hopes for a Silver Jubilee Exhibition of her
daughter's work. Over the last year, however, Mrs
Dacre's health has deteriorated to such a degree that I
believe she came to think that she would not live to see
it. So, when she came to me last autumn with the
suggestion that the Exhibition should be held this year,
I was quite ready to agree. Mrs Dacre has been most
generous to our College. She has endowed five annual
scholarships for further studies, which has meant that
some of our most promising students have been able to
go abroad after leaving us, when they would not normally
have been able to afford to do so."

"So what was the next step, after you had agreed?"

"Various bits of red tape—obtaining permission
from the Education Authority, for example. It all took
time. And then, in January, we started to run the
advertisements in the local paper."

"Requesting the loan of paintings?"

"Yes."

"Why not in the national press?"

Johnson sighed, sat back and folded his arms.
"Unfortunately Annabel Dacre was not well known,
though in the last year or two the value of her paintings
has soared. But when she was alive most of her pictures
were sold to local people—friends, neighhbours. Many
of them have scattered, of course, moved away, and we

did in fact insert two advertisements in the national dailies, but the bulk of her work is still hanging in houses locally. So we ran the advertisement in the *Gazette* fortnightly from the beginning of January to the end of March. By then the catalogues had to go to the printers, of course."

"And you got a good response?"

"Very good. Twenty-four paintings, which was, I confess, more than I had hoped for. Some of them from quite interesting sources."

"Do you remember a Mrs Holmes?"

"Ah yes, now that was a case in point—the painting had been bought by the girl's mother, stored away in an attic for . . ." He stopped, abruptly. "My God," he said. "I've only just made the connection . . . Mrs. Holmes . . . that girl who was murdered . . ."

"Yes," Thanet said heavily. "That's why I'm here. Though I would be grateful if you could keep this visit to yourself, at least until the case is solved." One can sound confident even if one doesn't feel it, he thought wryly as Johnson hastened to assure him of his discretion.

"Did you have much contact with Mrs Holmes?" Thanet asked.

"No. I saw her twice, once when she brought the picture in for authentication—it was one of Dacre's best, by the way. *The Cricket Match.*"

"Yes, I've seen it."

"And then of course I saw her briefly at the Private View. With her husband. The place was very crowded and I soon lost sight of them."

"You didn't notice anything unusual, out of the way, that evening?"

"No. I was terribly busy talking to people. I tried to get around to everybody, but it was such a crush. There really was a gratifying amount of interest in this exhibition. So often one feels like a voice crying in the wilderness . . ."

"I assume you have a list, of the people who were invited to the Private View?"

"Yes. In my office, at the College. No, wait a

minute, I think my rough copy might still be in my briefcase. Would you like to see it?"

"I'd like to borrow it, if I may."

Johnson seemed rather taken aback. "Oh. Oh dear, I do hope there won't be any . . . but still, I suppose we must try to . . . very well. I'll go and see."

He returned a few moments later, list in hand. "I brought a catalogue, too, Inspector, in case you might find it useful."

"Very kind of you. Thank you." He took the proffered papers, glanced at them, then stowed them carefully away in his inside breast pocket. "There's just one other point, Mr Johnson. Someone showed me one of the catalogues the other day, and the biographical notes on the back mention Annabel Dacre's 'tragic death.' What exactly does that mean? What did she die of?"

They were walking towards the door and now Johnson stopped dead. "Dear oh dear, Inspector. You mean you really don't know?"

"Know what?" Thanet asked—and thought, later, that he should have foreseen, by the glint of amused malice in the man's eyes, what the answer was going to be.

"That Annabel Dacre was murdered. And what is more, Inspector, her murderer was never found."

9

There had to be a connection between the two murders, Thanet told himself as he waited impatiently for the file on Annabel Dacre to be unearthed and brought to him. There just had to be. The link was too obvious for it to be otherwise. Somehow the events which led up to Julie's death had been triggered off at that Private View. But how?

Lineham had left a message saying that he had gone out to join the others in the second round of house-to-house enquiries. No witness had yet come forward in response to the radio and newspaper appeals put out in an attempt to confirm Kendon's story. Nor had there yet been any success in tracing the whereabouts of Horrocks, the salesman. So far they had not appealed for him by name. Thanet was always reluctant to advertise the names of witnesses except in cases of extreme urgency. The public always seemed ready to jump to unpleasant conclusions and it was all too easy for innocent people to suffer from such publicity. Besides, Horrocks was due back from his trip some time over the weekend and could be interviewed then. And now ... well, if Thanet's hunch was correct, most of the enquiries put in train so far could be irrelevant and all three suspects in the clear.

When the file arrived he had to restrain himself from snatching it from the man who brought it.

Annabel Dacre, he learnt, had been murdered on the evening of November 18, 1960. The same date, surely, on which Julie's father had been killed? Thanet suppressed the urge to check and read on. She had been found battered to death in her studio at the West Lodge, Champeney House, Little Sutton at 8.45 pm by Jennifer Parr, who had called the police. Julie's mother, Thanet thought excitedly. It was established that death had occurred between 7.45 and 8.45 pm, the vicar having spoken to Miss Dacre by telephone at the former time. Thanet paused at the name: the Reverend W. Manson. He took the catalogue and invitation list from his pocket, checked. Yes, as he had thought, it was on both lists.

As he read on carefully through the first pages of the bulky file the picture of what had happened on that foggy November day twenty years ago began to emerge.

Jennifer Parr and Annabel Dacre had been close friends. At three o'clock in the afternoon of November 18, Jennifer received a telephone call informing her that her husband had been seriously injured in a road accident and had been taken to Sturrenden General Hospital. He had been driving the Parrs' only car and as there would be no bus until half past four Jennifer had appealed to Annabel for help: could she run her into Sturrenden and look after Julie while Jennifer stayed at the hospital with her husband?

Annabel had agreed at once. She picked up Jennifer and Julie, drove them to the hospital and then took Julie home with her, having made Jennifer promise to ring her when she wanted to return home again. She would, she assured Jennifer, keep Julie for the night if necessary. She had done so on the odd occasion in the past and had installed her own old cot from the nursery at Champeney House in the corner of her studio, for this purpose.

At 7.45 pm David Parr died and shortly afterwards Jennifer began ringing Annabel. There was no reply. By ten past eight, knowing that Annabel should be at home looking after Julie, Jennifer, already in a state of shock over her husband's death, was beginning to feel panicky. She rang for a taxi which, owing to the fog, took twenty-five minutes to do the ten-minute journey, arriving at West Lodge at 8.45. The front door stood wide open and Jennifer, more uneasy than ever, asked the taxi driver to accompany her to the studio upstairs.

She found Annabel dead on the floor of the studio, the back of her skull smashed in, and Julie huddled in a corner of the cot which had, fortunately for the child, been placed in an alcove at the far end of the studio. Curtains had been partly drawn across in front of it, presumably to screen Julie from the light and enable her to go to sleep.

The police, however, were satisfied that although the murderer had presumably been unaware of Julie's presence, Julie would have been able to see what had happened. The theory that the child had actually witnessed the murder seemed to be confirmed by the fact that she was in a state of shock and unable to speak, a condition which lasted for several days. When she did recover she seemed to have no recollection whatsoever of what had happened.

Satisfied that Jennifer Parr had been under the eye of independent witnesses from three o'clock that afternoon until the discovery of the body and worried for the safety of the little girl, the police had advised Mrs Parr to leave the area at once. At no time, even at the inquest at which Jennifer Parr of course had to give evidence, had the fact of Julie's presence in Annabel's studio at the time of the murder been made public.

So. Thanet sat back and thought. Here, then, he was certain, was the source of Julie's nightmares. The cage was the cot in which Julie had been trapped during what must have been a terrifying experience.

Say, then, that the murderer had been someone known to Julie, say that, unable to cope with the memory of what she had seen, Julie had "forgotten" it completely, wiped it out of her conscious mind. And then suppose that years later she sees the murderer again, but without conscious recognition? The experience might well reactivate those suppressed memories, bring them nearer the level of consciousness in dreams,

nightmares in which Julie would experience once more
the terror buried deep for so long.

There was an awful lot of supposing and speculation in all this, Thanet thought. Surely, for example,
Julie would not have recognised the murderer, after all
these years? But it wouldn't have been necessary, as he
had already thought, for Julie actually to have recognised
him. There would just have had to be something—a
look, a gesture, an expression—which would activate
the memories buried deep in her subconscious, causing
them to work their way upwards, nearer to the surface
of her mind and make their presence felt in those
nightmares. Julie would have been bewildered, frightened,
aware that something was disturbing her without having
any idea of its real nature. Above all, she would have
been off balance, vulnerable.

But what about the murderer? It was equally unlikely,
surely, that he would have recognised, across a crowded
room, a child he hadn't seen for twenty years? Thanet
frowned, considering. Unless . . . unless Julie looked very
like her mother at the same age? Jennifer Parr had
been twenty-five at the time of Annabel's murder and
Julie had been twenty-three when she died. Mother
and daughter resemblances are often striking. Perhaps
it had been so in this case. Holmes would probably
know.

Thanet picked up the telephone and dialled Holmes's
number. No reply. Perhaps he had taken Thanet's advice and gone back to work? Thanet rang the supermarket.
This time he was in luck. After a few minutes Holmes
came on the line. His response to Thanet's question
was puzzled but immediate. Julie had been the "spitting
image" of her mother. Holmes had seen photographs of
Mrs Parr as a young woman and you would have
thought they were photographs of Julie, if it hadn't
been for the difference in the clothes.

Thanet replaced the receiver with satisfaction. So
far, so good. The next step would be to check which of
the original suspects of Annabel's murder had attended
the Private View. It would then be a matter of narrowing

Introducing the first and only complete hardcover collection of Agatha Christie's mysteries

Now you can enjoy the
greatest mysteries ever written
in a magnificent
Home Library Edition.

Discover Agatha Christie's world of mystery, adventure and intrigue

Agatha Christie's timeless tales of mystery and suspense offer something for every reader—mystery fan or not—young and old alike. And now, you can build a complete hardcover library of her world-famous mysteries by subscribing to The Agatha Christie Mystery Collection.

This exciting Collection is your passport to a world where mystery reigns supreme. Volume after volume, you and your family will enjoy mystery reading at its very best.

You'll meet Agatha Christie's world-famous detectives like Hercule Poirot, Jane Marple, and the likeable Tommy and Tuppence Beresford.

In your readings, you'll visit Egypt, Paris, England and other exciting destinations where murder is always on the itinerary. And wherever you travel, you'll become deeply involved in some of the most ingenious and diabolical plots ever invented ... "cliff-hangers" that only Dame Agatha could create!

It all adds up to mystery reading that's so good ... it's almost criminal. And it's yours every month with The Agatha Christie Mystery Collection.

Solve the greatest mysteries of all time. The Collection contains all of Agatha Christie's classic works including *Murder on the Orient Express, Death on the Nile, And Then There Were None, The ABC Murders* and her ever-popular whodunit, *The Murder of Roger Ackroyd.*

Each handsome hardcover volume is Smythe sewn and printed on high quality acid-free paper so it can withstand even the most murderous treatment. Bound in Sussex-blue simulated leather with gold titling, The Agatha Christie Mystery Collection will make a tasteful addition to your living room, or den.

Ride the Orient Express for 10 days without obligation.
To introduce you to the Collection, we're inviting you to examine the classic mystery, *Murder on the Orient Express*, without risk or obligation. If you're not completely satisfied, just return it within 10 days and owe nothing.

However, if you're like the millions of other readers who love Agatha Christie's thrilling tales of mystery and suspense, keep *Murder on the Orient Express* and pay just $9.95 plus postage and handling.

You will then automatically receive future volumes once a month as they are published on a fully returnable, 10-day free-examination basis. No minimum purchase is required, and you may cancel your subscription at any time.

This unique collection is not sold in stores. It's available only through this special offer. So don't miss out, begin your subscription now. Just mail this card today.

☐ Yes! Please send me *Murder on the Orient Express* for a 10-day free-examination and enter my subscription to <u>The Agatha Christie Mystery Collection</u>. If I keep *Murder on the Orient Express*, I will pay just $9.95 plus postage and handling and receive one additional volume each month on a fully returnable 10-day free-examination basis. There is no minimum number of volumes to buy, and I may cancel my subscription at any time.   70110

Name_____

Address_____

City_____ State_____ Zip_____

QB123
Send No Money...
But Act Today!

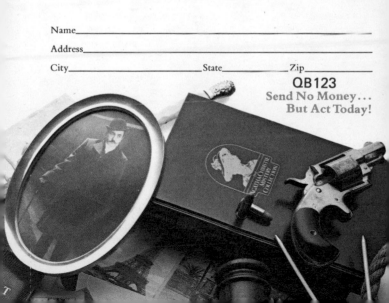

down the field by an examination of their movements
on the night Julie had died. With the exhibition catalogue and the Private View invitation list spread out
beside him he began to skim quickly through the
reports of interviews with witnesses. Details could wait
until later. First, he wanted to know how far his theory
held up.

It was a relatively simple matter to pick out the
names of the main suspects in the Dacre case. They had
all been interviewed over and over again. It was, however,
somewhat disconcerting to find that there were so
many—five, in all. Thanet's excitement mounted as,
one by one he checked them off on his lists and
discovered that four out of the five had loaned paintings
to the Exhibition and had therefore automatically received invitations to the Private View. It really was
beginning to look as though he might be right. With
any luck he might even be able to kill two birds with
one stone and track down a double murderer!

His stomach gave a protesting rumble and he
glanced at his watch. Half past one. He'd have a quick
bite to eat, then settle down to study the file in detail.
He frowned. For some time now he'd had a nagging
feeling that there was something he'd forgotten to do.
What could it be? Stiff from sitting so long in one
position he flexed his back. The twinge of pain reminded
him what it was. He'd had an appointment with the
physiotherapist at twelve. He must ring and apologise
at once. Joan would be furious that he'd forgotten.

During lunch he brooded over what he had learnt.
After that initial pang of pity and sorrow at his first sight
of Julie's dead body his attitude to her murder had
been intellectual. It was a puzzle to be solved, a jigsaw
to be assembled, a challenge against which he must pit
his wits. Now he found that in the light of this new
knowledge his feelings towards the case and above all
towards Julie had changed.

To begin with, what sort of an effect would the
witnessing of a brutal murder have had on a child of
three? Thanet thought of Sprig, and shuddered. Would

Julie have understood what she had seen? Probably
not, he decided, but she must have sensed the violence
in the air, have been terrified by the attack itself and by
the sight of the bloody mess that had been the back of
Annabel's head, frightened out of her wits by being left
alone in relatively unfamiliar surroundings with only
Annabel's body for company. She could have had to
wait for anything up to an hour before her mother
arrived, and to a frightened child even a minute must
seem sixty seconds too long.

Small wonder, then, that Julie had unconsciously
opted to "forget" the whole affair, scarcely surprising
that the police had deliberately suppressed any mention of her presence at the scene of the murder, and
understandable that her mother had whisked her off to
the anonymity of London, had given her to understand
that they had never lived anywhere else and had hid-
den that painting away in the attic.

Mrs Parr must have thought that once those early
nightmares ended—and Thanet had no doubt that they
had been very similar in content to the ones Julie had
recently experienced—that Julie had completely recovered
from her horrific experience. But Thanet was beginning
to believe that it had marked Julie for life, making her
terrified of emotion and cutting her off from the prospect of ever making satisfying relationships. A part of her
had, like Annabel, died that night and had never been
able to come to life again. Fanciful? he asked himself.
Perhaps. But he felt it explained so much about Julie
that had hitherto puzzled him.

Julie hadn't really had a chance. Too late, now, to
give her one, but not too late perhaps to fight back on
her behalf, to track down the person who had crippled
her mind and, if Thanet were right, had finally destroyed
her body too.

He headed back to his office with a new sense of
determination. Lineham was waiting for him. Thanet
took one look at him and said, "Bad morning?"

"Very frustrating. Nothing new at all. And no
whisper yet of the girl Kendon claims to have seen.

There were plenty of women between the ages of fifteen and thirty-five, of course, but none who fitted the bill. We asked about women who were visiting in the area that evening too, but with no luck. The girl could live anywhere in Sturrenden, of course, and if so, we'll just have to hope she comes forward in response to the appeals."

"Any news of Horrocks yet?"

"Not so far. He's expected home some time tomorrow, though, so we should be able to get hold of him then."

"Right. Well come on, sit down. There have been developments."

Lineham listened attentively while Thanet outlined his discoveries of the morning.

"You can read it all up for yourself later, of course," Thanet finished up, "but what do you think?"

Lineham's pleasant face was troubled. "Don't you think it's a bit, well, far-fetched, sir?"

Thanet was as taken aback as if a pet mouse had bitten him and said sharply, "Far-fetched? What do you mean, far-fetched?"

Lineham flushed and said defensively, "You did tell me yesterday to say what I really thought."

The pigeons were coming home to roost with a vengeance, Thanet thought. "You're quite right, of course, I did," he said, more gently. "So go on, tell me what you mean."

"Well, here we are with three perfectly good suspects, Holmes, Parrish and Kendon. I know we're not getting anywhere at the moment . . ."

"Dead right, we aren't."

"But that's always happening," Lineham went on doggedly. "Sooner or later, with any luck, we'll get a break. Kendon's witness will turn up, Horrocks might come up with something new. . . . Whereas this theory, well yes, I admit it seems possible that Julie Holmes and Annabel Dacre were murdered by the same person, but isn't it much more likely that Julie was killed by someone who was involved with her now?"

"Why? If the motive is powerful enough . . . It's

common knowledge that when someone has killed once he will find it easier the second time. Just think, man. This killer has been safe for twenty years and suddenly, bang, his security is threatened. He sees the girl who witnessed the first murder, a girl he thought never to see again, he recognises her, is pretty certain she has recognised him. Isn't it logical that he'd try and get rid of her?"

"But sir, with respect, there's an awful lot of assumptions there. You're assuming he recognised her, assuming he thought she'd recognised him and, most important of all, assuming he knew she'd witnessed the murder. How could he have known that, why should he have thought that she was any danger to him at all? From what you say, Julie's presence in the Dacre woman's studio was a closely guarded secret. The police kept quiet about it, Mrs Parr took her away, right after the murder, and I should think everyone thought what they were supposed to think, that she'd gone away because the double shock of her husband's death and her friend's murder, both on the same day, had been too much for her. I really can't see why, even if the murderer did recognise Julie at the Private View, he should have thought she was any threat to him."

"All right," Thanet said, "I admit there's a doubt there. But it could have happened. The murderer could have found out, afterwards, quite by chance, that Julie was in the studio that night. Someone could have seen Annabel Dacre with the child, going into West Lodge, have mentioned it later, in casual conversation. She herself might even have mentioned that she was looking after Julie to the vicar, when he rang that evening to ask for news of Julie's father. News gets around in villages, almost as if it is carried on the wind from one house to another. The murderer might not have known at the time that Julie was there, but that doesn't mean he might not have found out later. Dammit, man, you must admit it's possible."

"I can see that." But Lineham was clearly not convinced. Thanet looked at him in exasperation for a moment or two and then said, "In any case, what have we got to lose, by trying to find out? You admit yourself that we've come to a dead end at the moment."

Grudgingly, Lineham agreed.

Thanet began to laugh. "You certainly took my advice seriously, yesterday. No, don't apologise! All in all, I prefer it this way. Livens things up a bit."

Lineham grinned.

"Good," Thanet said briskly. He picked up his sheet of scribbled notes. "Now then, I think the first thing is to find out exactly where these people are living now. Unfortunately their addresses are not on this rough list of Mr Johnson's, and I don't suppose for a moment they'll all still be living in Little Sutton."

"No." Lineham was clearly now giving the matter his full attention. "Highly unlikely, I should think. A murder in a village, the murderer never found. People would have been bound to know who the main suspects were and life couldn't have been very comfortable for them, knowing that people were watching them, wondering if they were guilty. It's not easy to live down a thing like that."

"No. So you'd better start digging. Try Johnson's secretary first, get her to go into the College today, if necessary. If you can't get hold of her, you'll have to ring Johnson again. He won't be very pleased, but it can't be helped. I don't really want to wait until Monday. If you can't get hold of either of them you'll have to use your own initiative."

"There were four names, you said?"

"Five suspects originally, three men and two women. Only four of them appear on both these lists. The fifth, a man called Peake, isn't on either of them. But I'd like you to check on him just the same."

"And the advertisement requesting the loan of paintings appeared in the national as well as the local press?"

"Yes. So you could find that these people are scattered all over the country. Some might still be around, though. One of them was the local doctor, a Doctor Plummer. It would have been difficult for him

to give up his practice and start all over again—it was a
family practice, too, so it's all the more likely he would
have stayed. And two of the other suspects were a local
builder and his wife, Roger and Edna Pocock. They
might well still be in the area. Anyway, here's the list.
I've written Johnson's number and his secretary's at the
top. I'm going to spend the rest of the afternoon
working through this file."

Thanet took a few minutes after Lineham left to
get his pipe drawing really well, then settled down to
read. It was tedious, painstaking work, even for someone as experienced as he. The different threads of the
case had to be teased out, woven together into a
recognisable pattern, reports and statements read and
reread until each slotted into its place in the design.
Thanet worked his way steadily through the whole file,
took a five-minute break and then went back to study in
turn each batch of statements relating to the main
suspects. These were a surprisingly disparate group of
people, the link between them apparently being that
they had all been members of the Little Sutton Dramatic
Society.

The murder of Annabel Dacre, he reminded himself as he began, had taken place between 7.45 and 8.45
pm.

First, there was Dr Gerald Plummer, then aged
twenty-eight and unofficially engaged to Annabel. On
the night of the murder he had taken evening surgery
from 5 to 6 pm, had done some paperwork and had
then had supper with his father who had recently had a
serious illness and was in the process of withdrawing
from the practice. They always ate early because the
housekeeper left at seven thirty.

At seven forty-five there had been a phone call
(confirmed) from the local midwife: one of Dr Plummer's
patients had gone into labour and there were complica-
tions. He had set off at once but had had a puncture
and had experienced difficulties in changing the wheel.
He had therefore not arrived at the patient's home
(normally some ten minutes drive away) until eight

forty-five. The local garage confirmed that the next day Plummer had called in with a punctured tyre, but there was no telling, of course, when or how the puncture had occurred or how long, if at all, the doctor had really been delayed. Plummer had denied that Annabel had ever given him cause for jealousy and had expressed total bewilderment at the motive for such a brutal and senseless crime.

A bit of a stuffed shirt? Thanet wondered, reading through the statements again. The trouble was that it was difficult to gauge what the man was really like from the formal language of the official documents. Thanet sighed, relit his pipe and turned to the next suspect.

This was Edward Peake, aged twenty-five, also a bachelor, and an optician's assistant. He had lodgings in Rose Cottage, a breakfast and evening-meal arrangement. He had had supper at seven. His landlady had recently had bronchitis and during her illness he had been in the habit of taking her dog for his evening walk. That evening he left at seven fifty, keeping the dog on the lead until he had reached the woods adjoining the grounds of Champeney House. He had then let it off the leash for a run and had, he claimed, lost it. He had blundered around calling and whistling, eventually giving up around eight twenty-five and arriving back home at eight forty. The dog had apparently been run over in the fog, its body being found in a ditch at the side of a road next morning.

The landlady was hot in Peake's defence. "A nicer, kinder, more considerate young man you couldn't wish to find."

But again, no alibi for the time of the murder.

The third male suspect was the builder, aged thirty and married. He was in much the same position as Plummer and Peake, the difference being that he should, if his arrangements had not gone awry, have had a comfortingly sound alibi. The Pococks had had supper at six thirty that evening because Pocock had an appointment with a client at seven thirty to discuss some alterations to a house which the client was buying some five miles away from Little Sutton. Pocock left just after seven, allowing plenty of time because of the fog. He claimed to have arrived at the house a few minutes early and waited in vain for the client to turn up. At nine he gave up, arriving home at nine twenty in a furious temper at his wasted evening. The client confirmed that the appointment had been made. Unfortunately he lived twenty miles away and, unfamiliar with the area, had lost his way in the fog in the maze of country lanes. Eventually he had given up, found his way back to the main road and returned home, ringing Pocock to apologise as soon as he got there, at ten.

Edna Pocock aged twenty-nine and the fourth suspect, was a different matter. Thanet was very interested to note that although she had at the time of the murder been confined to bed, having had a miscarriage three days before, the police had obviously not ruled her out as a suspect. Why? Thanet found himself becoming increasingly impatient with the bald facts presented by the statements. He read on.

Edna Pocock had had two days in bed and on Friday, the day of the murder, had got up for the first time in the late afternoon, going back to bed immediately after supper, when her husband left for his appointment. According to her doctor (Plummer) she had still been very weak at the time. In any event, she, too, had no alibi for the time of the murder.

Finally, there was Alice Giddy, aged twenty-five. She lived with her mother, Mrs Florence Giddy, and worked in Cooper's, a department store in Sturrenden which had had a reputation for high quality merchandise and which, Thanet remembered, had given up the ghost ten years or so ago, when Marks and Spencer had opened a branch in the town.

On the night of Annabel's murder Alice Giddy had arrived home from work at six to find that her mother had unwisely attempted to hang some curtains and had had a fall, twisting her ankle. Alice had decided that the sprain was not bad enough to warrant calling the doctor and had spent some time dealing with the matter herself, treating the ankle with cold compresses and binding it up. She had then cooked the supper which her mother had partially prepared earlier in the day and they had eaten at seven fifteen. Mrs Giddy had been due to do the Church Flowers next morning and had fussed and fussed over the fact that now she wouldn't be able to. Nor could Alice do them after work the following day, Saturday, as she had already made arrangements to go to the theatre in London with friends. So, after supper, Alice had set off for the church at around seven forty-five, and had spent an hour doing the flowers and had arrived back home at eight fifty, having seen no one.

And that was it. Not one of the people whom the police had apparently suspected of having committed the murder had an alibi which would stand up, and no amount of patient digging had been able to confirm or to disprove any one of them. It had been a foggy November evening and people had not gone out unless they had to. Those who had had seen nothing of any significance.

Thanet pushed the file away and glanced at his watch. Five o'clock. He stood up and stretched. His back protested and, simultaneously, he experienced a twinge of guilt. Joan really would be furious, when she discovered that he had skipped his appointment.

He walked stiffly across to the filing cabinet, stretched out his arms to grasp two of the drawer handles at chest level, positioned his feet carefully and then, rising on tip-toe, arched himself over backwards as far as he could go, held the position for a count of three, returned to an upright position and relaxed. He repeated the exercise three times and then, feeling virtuous, returned to his desk and asked for some tea to be sent in.

Deliberately, while he sipped it, he kept his mind blank, giving his mental processes a necessary few minutes in which to recuperate. Then he swivelled his chair around, upturned the waste-paper basket, put his

feet on it and leaning back, closed his eyes—a position
strictly forbidden by his physiotherapist but most condu-
cive to constructive thinking.

There had been no circumstantial evidence against
any one of the suspects. Fingerprints of all of them had
been found in the studio, but this information had
proved worthless; rehearsals had often been held there.
There had been so sign of a forced entry to the Lodge.
Annabel had apparently let the murderer in herself and
taken him up to the studio. The murder weapon had
been a rough chunk of quartz which normally stood on
one of the studio shelves. Either, then, the murderer
had known of its being there and had counted on using
it, or the murder had been unpremeditated and the
rock seized as the nearest weapon to hand. There was
no way of telling. For all the physical evidence Annabel,
like Julie, could have been killed by a ghost.

Thanet could sympathise with the investigating
officer. It was obvious from the file that the police had
done their job with meticulous care. It must have been
galling to fail. Thanet did not recognise the name of the
man who had been in charge of the case—probably he
had retired long ago. A pity, he thought. It would have
been useful to discuss it with him.

On impulse he rang through to records, asked
them to check. He was in luck. Sergeant West, to
whom he spoke, was an older man and remembered
Detective Chief Inspector Low. Low had retired about
ten years ago, having transferred to Ashford some years
previously.

"Could you get me his address?"

"Ashford might have it, sir, unless he moved right
away when he retired. I'll check and ring you back."

Thanet replaced the receiver. It would certainly
help to talk to Low. Low would have known all the
people involved in the Dacre case, would be able to put
flesh on the bones of what Thanet had learnt.

Lineham came in and plumped down wearily in a
chair.

Thanet grimaced in sympathy. "Hard time?"

Lineham nodded. "Johnson's secretary was out for the day, her daughter said. I couldn't get hold of Johnson, either. Anyway, I've got all of them but Alice Giddy. Two of them were easy—well, three, assuming the Pococks are still together. Their number and Dr Plummer's were in the telephone directory. He's still in Little Sutton, but they've moved to Sturrenden. Little Mole Avenue."

"Ah yes. That's right on the edge of town, off the Canterbury Road, isn't it?"

"Yes. Both Peake and Giddy were much more difficult. Neither was in the directory. I rang Parry's, where Peake worked, and they confirmed that he'd left the area to go North, years ago. Well, to cut a long story short, he's dead, about five years ago, of a heart attack."

"That's definite?"

"Yes. I spoke to his last employer."

"Well at least that's one fewer to worry about. But you still haven't traced Alice Giddy?"

"Nope. She's probably moved away too. Short of going out to Little Sutton and asking questions, we'll just have to wait until we can get hold of Johnson's secretary."

"I don't want to do that—go out to Little Sutton, I mean. I'd like to catch all these people completely unprepared. I should think the murderer believes himself to be absolutely safe."

"If he is one of them."

"Yes, of course," Thanet was startled. He was so convinced by now that they were working on the right lines that he had forgotten Lineham's scepticism.

The telephone rang. Sergeant West had got hold of ex-D.C.I. Low's address and telephone number.

Thanet thanked him warmly. "Low was in charge of the Dacre case," he explained to Lineham. "He's retired, lives out at Biddenden, apparently." He dialled Low's number.

Low couldn't see Thanet that evening but readily agreed to an interview next morning. This suited Thanet very well. It had been a long day and he felt stale, semi-stupified by all the new information he had assimilated. He would prefer to be fresh and alert before interviewing any of these new suspects and as it would obviously be sensible to delay doing so until after he had seen Low, he now had the perfect excuse for going home. "While I'm seeing Low you can get hold of Alice Giddy's address from Johnson's secretary," he said to Lineham.

He shuffled together the loose papers from the Dacre file and pushed the folder across the desk. "Here you are," he said with a grin. "Your book at bedtime."

10

He was in a pit and he had to get out. Sprig was in danger, he knew it. He had to save her. He hurled himself frantically at the sides of his prison, seeking a toe-hold, finger-hold, anything by which he could lever himself upward, but there was nothing. The walls were soft, resilient, yielding beneath the pressure of his fingers. He looked up and saw suddenly that far, far above him there seemed to be some kind of ledge. Gathering together all his strength he sprang, the soft, furry surface receiving him suffocatingly into its embrace. And then he was free, the walls of the room soaring above him into darkness. They were hung with paintings and he knew at once where he was: Annabel's studio. And there, on the floor was Julie, long golden hair matted with blood. In the corner of the room stood a cot and he understood now his desperate sense of urgency. Sprig was in it and he had to get her away. He tried to hurry towards it but his legs were leaden. He could see Sprig now, clinging on to the bars of the cot, her eyes dilated with shock and terror. Just before he reached her he knew, without looking around, that the murderer was behind him. He spread his arms to protect her, but the murderer seized one of them, began to drag him away. . . .

He opened his eyes. Sprig's face floated before him, puckered with anxiety, and for a moment he hovered between nightmare and reality, uncertain which was which. Then she released his arm, at which she had been tugging, raised her eyebrows comically.

"OK, love," he whispered. "I'm awake now. I'll be out in a minute."

Satisfied that their morning ritual was under way she trotted off towards the door.

Already the nightmare was fading, but the sense of distress still lingered and Thanet deliberately held on to his dream, forcing himself to remember, to try to interpret. That pit . . . the pit in Johnson's studio, of course. And Sprig had been Julie, Julie Annabel . . . He almost groaned aloud. What a mess.

But Sprig would be waiting. Silently, he slid out of bed.

"I forgot to ask," Joan said suddenly, at breakfast. "How did you get on with Mrs James yesterday?"

"I didn't. No," Thanet held up a hand, "please, darling, listen. I honestly didn't have time. But I did ring to apologise." He didn't mention the fact that the apology had been made long after the appointment should have been kept, that he had clean forgotten about it.

"But you promised. . . ."

"I know. And I'm sorry, honestly. But so much happened yesterday."

"Bridget hurt her knee," Sprig announced, displaying the injury.

Thanet seized thankfully on the diversion. "Oh dear. How did that happen?"

"Luke Thanet, you are trying to change the subject," Joan said accusingly.

"So I am!" he said in mock astonishment.

"You did make a further appointment, I hope?"

"Well, as a matter of fact I was wondering if it was really necessary. My back's so much better now. . . ."

"Oh Luke, no! You can't sign off until she thinks you're ready."

"Well. . . ."

"Darling, please!"

Thanet sighed. "All right. I'll make one more appointment—just one, mind, and that'll be it."

"See what she says," Joan said vaguely. "Come on now, Ben, one more spoonful."

Ben obliged by scooping up some cereal and then, leaning over the side of his high chair, dropping it on the floor.

"Ben! Naughty boy!" Joan jumped up, fetched another spoon, closed Ben's cereal-covered fingers around it. "Come on now, darling, just one more spoonful. In your mouth," she added warningly. Then she fetched a piece of kitchen roll to mop up the mess.

"I shouldn't bother," Thanet said, watching her. "What's the point? He'll only do it again."

Obligingly Ben did, the cereal this time narrowly missing the top of Joan's head. "Ben!" she said and, catching Thanet's eye, began to laugh.

The little incident somehow succeeded in finally banishing the last of the shadow which had lingered as an aftermath of his nightmare and Thanet felt cheerful as he set off for the interview with Low. It was a glorious morning. A few fluffy white clouds enhanced the forget-me-not blue of the sky and the sun shone down upon a countryside clothed in the freshest and most delicate shades of green.

As soon as Thanet turned off the main road he found himself in narrow, winding lanes bordered on each side by a froth of Queen Anne's lace. He remembered the heady scent of it from earlier expeditions to the country and he wound down his window, inhaling the fragrance which drifted into the car. He found himself wishing that Joan were with him and remembering his resolution of a few days earlier to take her for a drive through the orchards. Here and there the apple blossom was already showing pink. Next Sunday, he promised himself, work or no work, they would have their expedition. If the weather were as good as this they might even take a picnic.

The prospect lifted his spirits still further and by the time he drew up in front of Low's bungalow he was feeling distinctly optimistic. It was, Thanet thought, rather an attractive bungalow. For himself, he preferred houses, but this one had some interesting features, being built entirely of stone in a style reminiscent of the Dordogne. He said so to Low, who had obviously been looking out for him; the front door opened before Thanet was half way up the path.

Low was delighted with Thanet's perception. "We felt it was the next best thing to the genuine article. We'd have loved to retire to the Dordogne—a surprisingly large number of English people do, you know—but family ties kept us here and now, well, we've settled and don't want to change." Low was a big man, a good sixteen stone, Thanet thought, and well over six feet. A luxuriant growth of white hair encircled a bald patch on the top of his head, sprouted from his eyebrows. Although he must now be well into his seventies his carriage was good, his flesh firm and well-muscled. Criminals, Thanet thought, must have found him a formidable opponent.

They chatted enthusiastically about the Dordogne (the Thanets had spent their honeymoon there) as Low led the way into a large, pleasantly furnished sitting room which overlooked the back garden. "Would you like some coffee, Inspector? I was just about to make some."

The coffee was good: hot and strong. How would it be, he wondered, when he and Joan were old? How would he feel about retirement? Would he simply feel that he had outgrown his usefulness, or would he be relieved that he could at last do all the things he never now had time for? He smiled to himself. He could just imagine Joan's reaction if he were saying all this to her. "We've got another thirty-odd years to get through first," she'd say. And of course she'd be right. It must be something about the atmosphere of this place . . .

"Right," Low said, seating himself opposite Thanet. "Now, it's the Dacre case you're interested in, you said?"

Thanet nodded. "Yes, I'll explain." Briefly he de-

scribed the progress of the Holmes case to date. Low
listened with complete attention, but it was not until
Thanet came to the link with the murder of Annabel
Dacre that he interrupted for the first time.

"Little Julie Parr!" he said.

Thanet could see from Low's face that he had
added two and two together and come up with the
same answer as Thanet. "Exactly," he said.

"I see," Low said slowly. "But . . . ? No, I won't ask
any questions until you've finished. Go on, please."

"I almost have. We've traced all the suspects but
Alice Giddy, and my sergeant's working on that now.
Peake is dead, by the way—five years ago, of a heart
attack. He moved up north soon after the murder."

"So now you'll be questioning them all about the
night of Julie's murder. Well, I wish you luck. She was a
sweet kid. To think he got her in the end . . ."

"He?"

Low shook his head. "A manner of speaking." He
stood up and walked restlessly across to the window. "I
never forgot the Dacre case." He looked back at Thanet
over his shoulder and gave a wry grin. "For one thing it
ruined my track record. We put everything we had into
that damned case, and all for nothing. So, if there's
anything I can do to help, anything at all . . ." he
returned to his chair, lifting his hands in a gesture of
largesse, "just ask."

"What I want from you really is the background to
the case—relationships, personalities, the sort of stuff
you can only guess at from reading the formal statements.
Together with your own feelings about the case. You
were there, you knew these people at the time. You'd
be bound to have a much better grasp of what was
going on between them than I could ever hope to attain
now, twenty years later."

"I don't know about that," Low said modestly, "but
I'll have a go." He leaned back in his chair, thrust his
hands hard down into the capacious pockets of the thick
knitted woollen jacket he was wearing, as if digging
deep into the past.

Then he relaxed, his eyes glazing with concentration. "It's a long time, of course, but since you rang last night I've been thinking, and it's all been coming back to me. The five suspects and Annabel Dacre were, as you've no doubt gathered by now, all members of the Little Sutton Dramatic Society, where they were on equal terms in a way they couldn't have been in everyday life. They came from very different classes. Annabel Dacre, of course, was the squire's daughter, from 'the big house' and as such one of the social queens of the district. Alice Giddy was closest to her, socially. Her mother was a wealthy widow and Annabel and Alice more or less grew up together—went to the same prep and boarding schools and shared an interest in art. Their paths divided when they left school. Annabel went on to study art in London and Paris while Alice had to stay at home. Her mother's health was deteriorating and she was insistent that Alice should live at home. They engaged a day companion for Mrs Giddy and Alice found herself a job."

"In Cooper's."

"That's right, in the fashion department. I can see you're wondering why she needed to work. The answer is that financially she didn't. I've no doubt at all that she took the job to get out of the house during the daytime. Mrs Giddy was an impossible woman, demanding, capricious. . . ."

"I thought she was hanging curtains on the day Annabel died. She sprained her ankle, didn't she? If she was sick . . . ?"

"Typical," said Low. "She'd do something like that—hang the curtains—just to make Alice feel guilty. She was furious that her daughter had refused to stay at home all the time and look after her. So she'd manoeuvre situations to make unpleasantness for Alice, even if it meant inconvenience for herself."

"You're not saying she'd actually go so far as to sprain her ankle . . . ?"

"No," though Low didn't sound too sure, "but she

certainly had no need to be climbing ladders, I assure you. She had a daily help as well as a companion."

"It's a wonder Alice didn't go to the Sturrenden College of Art," Thanet said, "if she was that keen."

"She did consider it, I believe, but rejected the idea—said she wasn't going to settle for the second-rate. She wanted to study dress design—had real talent, I believe."

"I don't suppose the Principal of the College of Art would be very flattered by that point of view!" Thanet said, with a grin.

Low returned the smile. "No. Anyway, the one bright spot in Alice's life, so far as I could see, was her fiancé, Gerald Plummer."

"Plummer! But I thought..."

"That he was engaged to Annabel? He was, at the time of her death, or so he claimed. Perhaps I should explain that Annabel Dacre was a very beautiful woman. Before she came back to Little Sutton and set up her studio in West Lodge after her years of study abroad, Alice Giddy and Plummer were always together. There was no formal engagement, you understand, but every last person in Little Sutton was convinced they'd marry and saw Mrs Giddy as the only obstacle to the union. Then Annabel came back and all of a sudden Alice was out in the cold. And make no mistake about it, she would care, would Alice. She might hide it, but she'd care all right."

"What was she like?"

"Tall, dark, elegant. Good-looking in an odd kind of way, but too intense for my taste."

"So Alice would have had motive, means and opportunity," Thanet said. "If she'd been awaiting her chance to take her revenge on Annabel—or perhaps merely to tackle her in private about Plummer—her mother's insistence on her doing the church flowers would have been a tremendous stroke of luck. A foggy night, an excuse to be out... She would have known about the chunk of quartz and no doubt Annabel would have let her in without hesitation...."

"Certainly. But unfortunately it's not quite as simple as that. The same could have been said of every other one of the four suspects."

"Every one?"

"Every single one," Low repeated firmly. "Plummer included. Let me explain: Annabel, as I said, was a very beautiful woman and very attractive to men."

"Didn't do her or Julie much good, did it? Almost makes me hope my daughter will grow up plain but worthy."

"Yes. Well, it seems to me that the main difference between them, from what you say, was that whereas Julie seemed unconscious of her power over men, Annabel positively revelled in hers. She had them all eating out of her hand, believe me, and the thing was, she was totally undiscriminating in the bestowal of her favours. One week it would be Plummer, the next Peake, the next Pocock. And so on, in various alternations. They couldn't have known where they were with her, any of them, and that's enough to drive any man mad, especially with a woman as beautiful as she was."

"Pocock was married, though."

"Didn't seem to make any difference. Annabel wasn't the first, as far as he was concerned, but way out of his class, really, and I don't think he'd have enjoyed being strung along. No, whoever did it, I think it may well have been Annabel's blow-hot, blow-cold technique which brought about her death."

"What about Pocock's wife? Why was she suspected? Surely, if she was used to her husband's affairs, one more wouldn't have made much difference?"

"This one might have been the proverbial straw that broke the camel's back. And in any case, Edna Pocock was in an unusually fragile state of mind. She'd just had a miscarriage—not the first, either."

"And that's another thing. Wouldn't she have been too weak, to get out of bed, walk to West Lodge in the fog—how far away was it, by the way?"

"About ten minutes walk from the village."

". . . walk to West Lodge, kill Annabel, walk back,

get rid of any evidence—blood stains, mud-stained shoes and so on—and be comfortably back in bed by the time her husband got home?"

"I agree it's unlikely," Low said, "but possible all the same. She had plenty of time. If I remember rightly, Pocock left home at about seven that evening and didn't get home until about half past nine."

"I only wish I had a memory like yours!" Thanet said. "To be able to remember a detail like that after twenty years..."

"Believe me, the facts of this case were burned on to my brain," Low said.

"What was she like, Edna Pocock? How long had they been married?"

"Ten years. Oh, she was small, plump, a motherly-looking type. Not terribly bright—not stupid, but just not very intelligent. I always hoped she might have managed to have children later, she seemed to me to be the sort of woman who would have made an excellent mother—warm, kind, comforting, you know?"

"What about Peake? I know he's out of it, but I'd still like to know."

"An entirely different type from Plummer. Now Plummer was tall, solid, a good family-doctor type, but Peake was thin, nervous, intense, the sort who would worship from afar, I should think."

"But Plummer? How would he have reacted to cavalier treatment?"

"Not well. I think there was a streak of vanity there. I think he rather enjoyed being a big fish in a little pond."

"Hmm. Well, here comes the sixty-thousand-dollar question. Who do *you* think did it?"

Low sat back in his chair, steepled his hands beneath his chin and looked back into the past. "Who do I think did it?" he murmured. He lifted his hands in a gesture of helplessness before letting them come to rest on the arms of his chair. "Well, for my money, Alice Giddy. But there is nothing, absolutely nothing to substantiate that suspicion."

"I realise that. I shouldn't have asked, I suppose," Thanet said. He tapped the burning ash from his pipe into the big ashtray, made sure it was safe before stowing it away in his pocket. "Well, I think that's about it for the moment, Chief Inspector."

"Mr.," said Low, with a rueful smile, "and it's been a pleasure. I hope you get him. He's had twenty years' grace already."

The burly figure, hand raised, remained reflected in Thanet's driving mirror until he turned the corner at the end of the road.

11

It was now ten-thirty and it occurred to Thanet that Little Sutton was only three or four miles out of his way. Suddenly he wanted to see it. He'd been there before, of course, in passing, but on those occasions it had been a village like any other, with no particular significance for him. Now he wanted to look at it in a different light, as the place where the Holmes case had really begun. And he'd like to see West Lodge, where Annabel had lived and died. . . .

He pulled up at the next telephone box.

"Mike? Thanet here. Any luck with tracing Alice Giddy?"

"Just got it." Lineham's voice was faint. "Hang on a minute."

"Can you speak up? This is a terrible line."

"I got Johnson's secretary to go in to the College and open up her files." Lineham's voice was still faint and Thanet pressed the receiver hard against his ear.

"She—Alice Giddy, that is, now lives in . . ." His voice faded out.

"Can you repeat that? Speak up, can't you? I can hardly hear you. Oh, Maddison House, you say. Where Parrish lives! That's interesting." Any connection there? he wondered.

Lineham's next words were unintelligible. It occurred to Thanet that there was no interference on the line, and that Lineham seemed perfectly to understand everything he said. "Mike, are you all right?"

"Yes, of course." The answer was clearer this time, as if Lineham had made an effort.

"Who else is in, this morning?"

"D.C. Bennet, D.C. Stout, D.S. Parkin . . ."

"Put Parkin on, will you? Parkin? What's the matter with Lineham. He sounds odd. Is he ill or something?"

"He won't thank me for telling you, sir, but we think he's got flu. He looks like death warmed up, and . . ."

The connection was cut. Thanet swore, dug out some more coins, dialled again. "Parkin? Now look here, I'm going to tell Lineham to go home. You make sure he does just that, will you? Now put him on."

The matter was soon settled. The token resistance Lineham put up showed Thanet just how ill his sergeant must be feeling. He knew himself how frustrating it was to have to pull out of a case just when things were getting really interesting. Thanet checked that nothing else of note had come in that morning and rang off.

He found Little Sutton without difficulty, but did not stop in the centre of the village. Hoping that his memory was serving him correctly he drove around the Green and out by a different road. Half a mile out of the village he smiled with satisfaction as a tall, crumbling red-brick wall came into view on his left. As he had thought, these were the grounds of Champeney House.

A hundred yards further on he pulled up in front of a pair of tall wrought iron gates. The drive beyond them, curling away into the distance and disappearing into an avenue of tall, dead elms, was obviously never used. Couch grass and other weeds had thrust their way up through the old tarmac which was visible only in crumbling patches. A small, stone-built lodge, solidly built but undoubtedly empty and neglected stood within the gates, to the right.

Thanet got out of his car, locked it and approached the gates. The words WEST LODGE were cut into the stone of the right-hand pillar. The gates, however, Thanet saw to his disappointment, were padlocked. Flakes of rust came off on his hands as he gripped them to peer through at the little house.

Weeds and overgrown shrubs grew right up to the walls, half covering the windows, and ivy climbed the walls unchecked, thrusting destructive fingers through rotting window frames, entwining gutters and drain-pipes in a stranglehold which must surely soon bring them down. Broken window panes gaped everywhere, hastening no doubt the process of decay by letting in the wind and rain. Thanet gave the gates one last, frustrated rattle and was about to turn away when he hesitated, stooped to examine more closely the tangled chain which had been loosely wound several times around the inmost bars of the gates. Surely that link should not be projecting like that? He began to fumble with the rusted links and almost at once saw with satisfaction that at some point long ago—for the ends had rusted over—someone had cut through the links and then twisted them around each other so that to a casual inspection they still appeared unbroken. It took him a few minutes to disentangle them, then he was through, pushing the gates roughly together behind him.

His hands were covered in rust and he bent to rub them impatiently on a clump of rough grass before pushing open the little wicket gate which led into the overgrown garden. Here and there a few flowers still survived: a sprawling, woody tangle of forsythia, a single peony thrusting its way up through a tangle of last season's dead foliage, a drift of bluebells carpeting the ground beneath an old apple tree at the far side of the garden.

Thanet approached the front door and pushed. It was, of course, locked. He picked his way around to the back of the house, pausing to peer into one of the front windows as he went. Here a surprise awaited him: the room was furnished—sketchily, true, but furnished nevertheless. For a moment he was afraid that the place was, despite all the signs, inhabited after all, but a second glance reassured him. That room had not been lived in for years. Annabel's mother, then, had presumably not bothered to clear the house after her daughter's death. Would Annabel's studio, like Miss Havisham's wedding feast, have been preserved intact over the years? The thought excited him.

At the back of the house he had better luck. As he had hoped, someone—children or courting couples perhaps—had been unable to resist the temptation of breaking in. When he put his shoulder to the door it yielded to him, its sagging timbers scraping protestingly over the stone threshold.

The dank, musty smell of a long-uninhabited house filled his nostrils as he stepped into a large, square kitchen with generous windows on two walls. Attempts had been made to modernise it, presumably when Annabel had come to live here: there was a stainless-steel sink, dull and dusty from disuse, and units with formica work surfaces along two walls. Out of curiosity Thanet opened one of the cupboards. Yes, as he had thought, the house had never been cleared. The decayed remains of cardboard packets mingled with liberal sprinklings of mouse droppings. A quick glance into some of the other cupboards told him that, predictably, everything of any value had long since been stolen.

It was the same story everywhere else on the ground floor. Even now, after all this time, lighter patches on the wallpaper showed where prints or pictures had once hung, and the only items of furniture which remained were those which would have been too cumbersome to move. Carpets and rugs had been taken, but curtains still hung at the windows, presumably to give the impression that nothing within had been disturbed. Empty Coca-Cola bottles and crumpled crisp packets showed that children had played here, no doubt relishing the atmosphere of strangeness and decay in games of mystery and adventure.

Treading gingerly for fear of rotting floorboards, Thanet began to move softly up the short, straight flight of stairs, his footsteps muffled by the rotting remnants of the stair carpet. Somewhere above him was Annabel's studio and his curious, irrational need to see it, his hope that it might have survived the depredations of the thieves who had more or less stripped the ground floor, caused his heart to beat faster, his breathing to become ragged.

And so his first reaction as he stepped into the long, narrow room which took up one half of the entire first floor and ran through from the front of the house to the back, was one of disappointment. Here, too, little had been left. A bulky button-backed settee, its linen covering discoloured and rotting, still stood beneath the front windows and a long deal table, its top liberally stained with faded splotches of paint, had obviously been dismissed as having no commercial value.

Thanet walked to the centre of the room, his footsteps sounding hollow on the bare floorboards, and then stood looking about him. The windows in the rear wall—the north wall, presumably—had been enlarged and the light was excellent. To the right of them was a deep alcove, the alcove in which Julie's cot must have stood. Thanet walked across to look at it. At one time it must, he decided, have been a dressing-room leading off the back bedroom. The dividing wall had been removed and then, perhaps at a later date, a ceiling curtain track installed. This was, no doubt, the very curtain which had saved Julie's life. Thanet fingered the rotting material and then grimaced, rubbing his hands on the seat of his trousers.

He turned away. There was nothing to be learnt here. If the ghosts of the past still lingered, they had nothing to say to him. He had done what he had wanted to do, however. He had seen the place where it all began, and some need in him was satisfied. He made his way softly down the stairs, shut the back door firmly behind him.

Back in the village people were just coming out of church. Thanet pulled into the kerb and watched them disperse, some by car and some on foot. Many of them no doubt would clearly remember the murder of Annabel

Dacre, some might even still mourn her. He waited
until the last car had driven away, then he got out of his
own, locked it and strolled across to the lych gate at the
entrance to the churchyard. The sun was warm on his
back as he turned to study the peaceful scene.

Little Sutton was a typical English village. There
was a large, roughly triangular area of somewhat ragged
grass, surrounded by a hotch-potch of houses, some
large, some small, reflecting the development of English architecture from Tudor times to the present day.
Tiny black and white timber-frame cottages rubbed
shoulders with Georgian aristocrats in mellow red brick
and the occasional Victorian upstart with its usual quota
of stained glass and dank evergreen shrubs. The only
modern house, a chalet bungalow with picture windows
and a green-tiled roof, had obviously been built in the
former garden of one such monster.

To one side of the Green were the two huge oak
trees which Thanet had recognised in *The Cricket Match*,
their massive trunks ringed with white wooden benches—
no doubt a favourite place for the older men of the
village to congregate on summer afternoons, thought
Thanet. But today, despite the sunshine, it was still too
chilly for anyone to be sitting about in the shade, and
the green was deserted except for a boy of about twelve
who was throwing sticks for his dog.

In a little while he would try to find Sutton House
and interview Dr Plummer, Thanet thought. Meanwhile the sleepy calm of the place had infected him and
without any conscious purpose he turned and strolled
into the churchyard, admiring the satisfying simplicity
of the Norman church tower, the mellowness of the
stone. A pity, he thought, that its setting was so unkempt.
The churchyard was large, many of its graves overgrown
with grass. An attempt had been made to tend a wide
swathe of ground on either side of the path, however,
and there was an area with well-tended graves and
modern headstones which was trim and neat.

Thanet left the path and began to wander about
amongst the older graves, pausing now and then to try

to read an inscription; many were quite illegible, worn away by centuries of wind and rain.

He had not yet admitted to himself what he was doing and it was not until he came across it that he knew. The grave cried out to be noticed, an island of order in the surrounding chaos.

ANNABEL DACRE
1935-1960
"Snatched away in beauty's bloom"

The grass was close-cut, the edges neatly trimmed, and in the centre of the rectangle was a perfect circle of miniature rose bushes, strong new shoots giving a promise of the flowers to come. Someone, even after twenty years, was still taking a good deal of trouble over Annabel's grave.

Who? Thanet wondered. Her mother? Remembering the Memorial Exhibition for a daughter twenty years dead, the pain which had caused Mrs Dacre to seal up Annabel's house and let it fall down rather than allow anyone else to live in it, Thanet could well imagine Annabel's mother making a regular pilgrimage to tend her daughter's grave.

"Beautifully kept, isn't it?" The voice behind him made him jump.

The woman was tall, almost as tall as Thanet, and thin, painfully so. The brown knitted suit she was wearing hung loosely on her, and her cream straw hat topped a face from which the flesh had melted away. Skin the colour of parchment accentuated the shockingly skull-like effect. Her eyes, however, were beautiful, a deep, delphinium blue and alert—disconcertingly assessing, Thanet felt, the effect her physical appearance was having upon him.

"Theodora Manson," she said, putting out her hand. "My husband is vicar here." Her hand in his felt as dry as a dead twig, as insubstantial as a dead leaf.

"Luke Thanet," he responded. He gestured at the

grave. "It's a long time for someone to have kept on coming, year after year, to keep it looking like this."

"Her mother does it," Mrs Manson said. "She's getting old now and she's had a lot of ill-health lately, but she still manages it somehow." She looked down at the grave. "Annabel was a lovely girl—beautiful, that is. And a very talented painter. Such a waste."

"I think I've seen one of her paintings," Thanet said. "A village cricket match." He nodded over his shoulder. "On the Green."

"Ah yes, I know the one you mean. I saw it at the recent exhibition of her work. You didn't go, I gather?"

"No, I'm afraid not. I didn't see the painting until after the exhibition was over, or I would have. I liked it very much."

"Would you like to see another of her paintings?"

Thanet concealed his surprise at the invitation. "Yes, I would. Very much."

"Come along, I'll show it to you. We're very proud of it. It's called *The Church Fête*, which was why I especially wanted it for my husband. I bought it for his birthday, the year before Annabel . . . died. It seemed a wicked extravagance at the time, but I've never regretted it. Apart from anything else, it has proved to be an excellent investment, though we don't think of it that way. We simply enjoy looking at it."

They turned on to a footpath which crossed the churchyard towards the high stone boundary wall. Mrs Manson led him through a rickety wooden gate into the vicarage garden. Thanet exclaimed in delight and Mrs Manson smiled with undisguised pleasure at his reaction.

"It's my hobby," she said.

Smooth green lawns stretched away on either side, bordered by curved flower beds packed with a profusion of shrubs and flowers. Thanet knew very little about gardening, but he could recognise the hand of an artist when he saw one, could appreciate the hard work and expertise behind an apparently casual yet perfect effect like this.

"It's beautiful," he said. "Really beautiful."

"I've worked on it for thirty years. I don't do the lawns, now, of course, but I still manage the rest somehow. Fortunately it doesn't need much maintenance. It's so stuffed with plants there's no room for weeds. We'll go in through the french windows," she said, setting off across the lawn towards the house.

The long windows stood open to the warmth of the midday sun and the scents of the garden. Thanet followed the tall, gaunt figure through a faded sitting-room into what was obviously the vicar's study. Mrs Manson gestured towards the painting. "We hung it where it gets the best light," she said.

Thanet stepped forward eagerly. This was the first of Annabel's paintings that he had seen properly. It was small, perhaps ten inches wide by eight inches high, and glowed on the pale wall like a jewel. Thanet leaned forward to examine it more closely. In brilliant, primary colours, Annabel had painted the village fête on the Green. There were the two tall oaks, the circular white-slatted benches, the scatter of houses set around the vivid emerald of the grass. The painting was crammed with detail—stalls, sideshows, red and white striped fortune-teller's tent complete with turbaned head protruding from between the flaps. And everywhere were people—buying, selling, talking, laughing, walking, gesticulating—tiny, stylised figures yet each uniquely individual.

"It's marvellous," Thanet said, meaning it. "Fascinating."

"That's me," said Mrs Manson with a smile, pointing to the turbaned head. "I used to be rather good at fortune-telling. Not particularly appropriate for a vicar's wife," she added with a gleam of amusement in her eyes, "but there we are. We have to use the talents God gives us, don't we? Especially when they bring in money to repair the church tower."

"She put real people into her paintings?" Thanet said with interest. "I didn't realise that."

"Oh yes, we're all there. That's my husband."

Mr Manson, sober in black suit and clerical collar, was bending over to comfort a sobbing child.

"Remarkable perception, Annabel had, for one so young."

The last words came out in a gasp and Thanet, turning sharply, found Mrs Manson supporting herself on the back of a chair, her lower lip drawn in and clamped between her teeth, her forehead beaded with sweat. He exclaimed in concern, helped her to a chair and lowered her gently into it.

"Can I get you something?"

She shook her head feebly. "No thank you. I'm so sorry. I'll be all right in a few minutes."

"A glass of water?" he persisted.

"No, really." She leaned back, closed her eyes, seemed to withdraw into herself, somewhere far away from him. Thanet stood awkwardly in front of her for a moment or two and then tiptoed softly to the door. It seemed rude, ungrateful to go without a word of thanks, but he felt that he had no right to intrude any longer. At the door he paused. Had she said something? He turned, found that she had rolled her head towards him, was looking at him.

"I'm sorry." The words were scarcely more than a whisper.

He was suddenly angry, at the pain she must be suffering and at her need to apologise. "Don't," he said fiercely and then, modifying his tone, "Thank you for showing me your picture. Are you sure there's nothing I can do for you?"

Her head moved slightly in a gesture of gratitude. "I'll be all right in a little while."

He raised his hand in farewell and then left, walking swiftly through the garden without seeing it, his mind a confused jumble of emotion—pity for Mrs Manson, whom he had liked, anger at his own helplessness, admiration for her stoicism, guilt at his deception. He was back at the lych gate before he realised that there was something else, too—frustration that their discussion of the painting had been interrupted. He would have liked to identify more of those tiny figures. Amongst them, quite possibly, had been the murderer.

The thought made him feel even more angry with himself. "Heartless pig," he muttered as he crossed the road towards his car. He had unlocked it before he realised that he had not yet finished his work here. He still wanted to see Dr Plummer.

He relocked the car and looked about. The boy and his dog had gone and the Green was deserted. Somewhere not too far away, though, someone was using a motor-mower. Thanet stood quite still, trying to detect the source of the sound. Then he set off across the Green.

In the garden of one of the little black and white cottages a young man, stripped to the waist, was cutting the grass. He switched off the machine, came to the gate. "Doctor Plummer?" He walked across the pavement and pointed. "That house. The big one with the white windows."

Thanet thanked him and walked on.

Sutton House was one of the classic Georgian ones. The man who opened the door was in his late twenties. "Doctor Plummer? I'm sorry, he's not here."

"I'm really very anxious to get in touch with him." Deliberately, Thanet did not yet identify himself. If he could get what he wanted without doing so, he would. No point in giving Plummer prior warning. "Will he be back, later?"

"I'm sorry, no. Actually, he's in hospital—went in just over a week ago. I'm standing in for him. Can I help you?"

"Thank you, but it's a personal matter," Thanet said. "Could you tell me which hospital?"

"Sturrenden General."

So, when Julie was murdered last Tuesday evening, Plummer had been in hospital. Easy enough to check, Thanet thought as he went back to his car. That left Alice Giddy and the two Pococks, out of the original five suspects. In the car he began to sing.

Things were definitely looking up.

12

A treat, Sunday lunch at home: roast beef, meltingly tender; roast potatoes, crispy on the outside, white and fluffy inside; white cabbage cooked in its own juices with chopped bacon and onions; individual batter puddings, as light as soufflés; thick, rich gravy and, finally, apple pie with cream. Thanet appreciated every mouthful. In the present economic situation this was a tradition which was becoming increasingly difficult to maintain, but he and Joan had agreed that however much they had to tighten their belts during the week they would keep it up as long as they possibly could.

Afterwards he was tempted to linger. The thought of a long lazy afternoon reading the Sunday papers, chatting to Joan, playing with the children, beckoned to him. He knew, however, that if he gave in to temptation the reality would not be like that. He would be restless, unable to settle down all the while he knew that there was work he should be doing. So when he had topped off the meal with a refreshing cup of tea he kissed Joan a reluctant good-bye and set off for Maddison House.

How the builders had ever managed to obtain planning permission to build the place was a mystery to him. There must, he thought, have been some palm-greasing somewhere. It was a single, ten-storey block of luxury flats which had been built in a wooded area about half a mile from the edge of Sturrenden. Clearly visible above the trees from some distance away, it looked as out of place as a beached whale. Thanet

looked about with interest as he emerged from the
approach road through the wood into the extensive,
cleared space around the building.

Neatly tended lawns and rose-beds, and well-placed
urns of velvety, wine-red wallflowers indicated that the
tenants of Maddison House employed a gardener who
was industrious if not inspired. Thanet bent to look
more closely at one of the elaborate lead urns, then
tapped it with his knuckles. He straightened up with a
grimace. Fibreglass, without a doubt. He didn't like the
spurious.

Wide glass doors led into a spacious hall floored
with black and white marble tiles. Against one wall was
a long oak table and on it a huge bowl of scarlet tulips.
Thanet remembered the caretaker (possibly cum-gardener)
that Parrish had mentioned. No doubt it was his job
and possibly his wife's, to give the place this groomed,
carefully-tended air and to keep it running smoothly
and efficiently.

Thanet consulted the wall indicator and discovered
that Flat 26 was on the seventh floor. He took the lift,
stepping out into a red-carpeted lobby some twelve feet
square with four front doors in it. He rang the bell of
Flat 26 and waited, conscious of the silence. There
must be dozens of people living in this place and yet so
far he had not seen or heard a single sign of life. What
did they all do on Sunday afternoons? Sleep?

As soon as the door of 26 opened, however, he
realised that the flats were extremely well sound-proofed;
waves of sound assailed his eardrums. He recognised
Beethoven's Pastoral Symphony. Alice Giddy obviously
had an efficient stereo system.

"Miss Giddy?" He looked at the woman before him
with interest. Tall, dark, elegant, Low had said. Good-
looking in an odd kind of way, but too intense for his
taste. Alice Giddy had not changed much, it seemed.
Almost as tall as Thanet, she was wearing a striking
dress—robe was perhaps a better word, Thanet thought—
in peacock blue, with a swirling, abstract design in
black from shoulder to hem. Her hair was short and

straight, glossy as a blackbird's wing and beautifully cut
to the shape of her neat head. Cool green eyes surveyed
Thanet from a face which reminded him of a Siamese
cat's in more than shape; it had the same quality of
independence, of indifference to the opinions of others.

"Yes?" she said, lifting her eyebrows in polite
enquiry.

He introduced himself, showed his identification at
her request. After a moment's hesitation she turned.
"You'd better come in."

The room into which she led the way was as
strikingly individual as Johnson's studio-cum-sitting-room.
The walls were chocolate brown and decorated with a
series of huge murals in swooping whorls of orange,
gold, purple and green. The carpet was thick, white,
shaggy and there was little furniture: a low glass-topped
table and two long, white leather sofas heaped with tiny
cushions in many colours, fabrics and shapes.

She crossed to the elaborate stereo system against
one wall and stopped the record on it before waving
him to one of the sofas. "Do sit down." She seated
herself opposite him, crossed her legs, folded her hands
neatly in her lap and waited. Her very lack of curiosity
or interest intrigued Thanet and warned him that he
would have to be very careful if he were not to lose
control of this interview. Certainly there would be no
question, with this woman, of setting her at her ease
and catching her off her guard or, for that matter, of
fobbing her off with evasions and half-truths. He decided to be as impersonal, as business-like as she.

"I'm here in connection with the murder of a girl
called Julie Holmes," he said, and watched carefully for
her reaction. As he had expected, she showed nothing
but faint bewilderment. One eyebrow arched.

"I'm sorry, Inspector, I really fail to see . . ."

"It will no doubt become apparent to you," he said
crisply. "Perhaps you would begin by telling me of your
movements last Tuesday evening."

She shifted her body slightly, a movement of
impatience. "Oh really, Inspector!"

"Please," he cut in again. "I can assure you I have a reason for asking." He was beginning to enjoy himself.

She raised one hand slightly, in a gesture of concession. "Very well. I'll go and fetch my diary."

She disappeared into an adjoining room, returned a few moments later with a large green leather-bound desk diary. She sat down, leafed through its pages in silence. "I'm afraid there's nothing of any use here. You can see for yourself." And she handed him the diary, open, with an "I've-got-nothing-to-hide" gesture.

Tuesday May 6 was blank. Thanet nodded acknowledgement and handed it back to her. "You really have no recollection? It is, after all, only five days ago."

She shrugged, impatient again. "As there's nothing in my diary, I assume that it must have been a perfectly ordinary day."

"Which means?"

"That I would have worked in the shop until five-thirty, then come home and spent the evening here."

"The shop?"

"My boutique in Sturrenden. TOPS."

Thanet had a quick mental image of the bag he had found in Julie Holmes's wardrobe. Purple, with TOPS in gold lettering on the side. Another connection . . . A thought struck him. Could he have been wrong? Could Julie have come face to face with the murderer not at the Private View, but in Alice Giddy's boutique? If so, he must now tread warily indeed.

"Which is why I'm here," he said, with a flash of inspiration. "Mrs Holmes was a customer of yours. We found one of the carrier bags from your shop in her wardrobe."

"Really?" Alice Giddy said, with indifference. "Is that so surprising? I should think there'd be one of our carrier bags in the wardrobe of many of the women in Sturrenden—or at any rate in the wardrobes of those who can afford us." And, for the first time, a glint of wry amusement showed briefly in her eyes. "I must say I'm surprised that an inspector, no less, should turn up on my doorstep to follow up so tenuous a link."

"You don't remember the girl?"

"What was she like?"

Thanet told her, but at the end of his description Alice Giddy shook her head. "I'm sorry. We have so many customers . . . and in any case I might well have been working in the office above the shop when she came in, in which case my assistant would have served her."

"Perhaps I could have your assistant's address," Thanet said, keeping up the fiction.

"By all means, though I really can't see much point." She dictated it to him and then leaned forward, preparatory to rising. "And now, if that's all, Inspector . . ."

"Not quite, I'm afraid. You still haven't told me how you spent last Tuesday evening." Even at the risk of looking ridiculous he had to persist.

She did not sit back again, but remained poised on the very edge of the settee. "I told you, I can't remember. I assume I spent the evening here, as usual."

"Alone?"

"Alone."

Thanet gave up. Clearly, there was no point in continuing. He stood up. "Very well."

Her eyes, looking up at him, mocked him, dared him to go on, to thank her for her help in the conventional way.

"If you remember later on, perhaps you could contact me." He took out his card and laid it on the glass-topped table.

"By all means," she said, uncurling herself. They stood for a brief moment facing each other across the low table, both of them paying tribute to a worthy adversary, before she turned, led the way to the door and showed him out.

In the car Thanet was thoughtful. Had he been right to switch his strategy like that when he had learnt that Alice was the owner of TOPS? He wasn't sure if it had been good tactics or a simple loss of nerve. It had suddenly seemed so much more likely that Alice Giddy was the murderer and if so he wanted not only more time to think but to keep as many cards up his sleeve as possible. As it was she was free to think that the police, at a loss how to proceed, were simply casting their net wildly in the hope of coming up with a useful lead. But she was no fool and if she were guilty and he had so much as mentioned the Dacre Exhibition she would have realised at once that he was on to the past link between Julie and herself.

Thanet began to feel depressed. Alice Giddy had impressed him. She would be a tricky adversary indeed. If she were guilty he could not imagine her admitting it even if the evidence were incontrovertible.

And, when it came down to it, what evidence was there, at the moment?

None. None whatsoever.

13

―■―■―■―■―■―■―■―■―

Fortunately there was no time for the depression to take too firm a hold upon him. The journey back into the town took only ten minutes and he had to put the interview with Alice Giddy firmly behind him and free his mind for his intended visit to the Pococks.

Little Mole Avenue was on the far side of Sturrend̲e̲n̲ and he decided to call in at the hospital ͏on̲ ͏i̲͏ ͏t̲h̲e̲n̲ check up on Dr Plumme͏r͏ ͏T͏ ͏o̲n̲ ͏t̲h̲e̲ way, to found, he͏e͏n͏ ͏a̲l̲l̲ ͏u͏c͏r͏. The doctor's stand-in had, he . ͏ ͏b̲e̲e̲n̲ telling the truth. Gerald Plummer had been admitted to the hospital on May 2, four days before the murder. On May 5, after two days of tests, he had undergone an operation, and was now convalescent. He had, moreover, been under constant supervision, having refused to go into a private room on the grounds that what was good enough for his patients ought to be good enough for him. It was out of the question that on May 6 he had been either fit enough or free to have been in Gladstone Road, committing a murder.

Thanet left, satisfied.

As he swung out of the hospital car park and into the Sunday quiet of the streets he reviewed what he knew of the Pococks. They had been slightly older than the rest of their little group at the time of Annabel's murder, Pocock being thirty and his wife a year younger, and they had been the only married couple involved. Pocock at that time had, according to Low, been a philanderer and Edna the complaisant (or ignorant)

wife. She had also been that eternally tragic figure, the
motherly woman who is denied children. What would
they be like now? How would the years have treated
them? Was Pocock now an ageing Don Juan, and would
his wife at last have found fulfilment in motherhood?

The answer to this last question was obvious the
moment Thanet pulled up outside the Pococks' house.
This was in a sedate neighbourhood of large Victorian
houses set in sizable gardens. Most of them, Thanet
thought, would probably now be divided up into flats,
having proved too expensive to run. The Laurels stood
out from its neighbours by virtue of its cluttered garden
and the noise which emanated from it. Thanet, standing
at the gate, counted five children of varying ages. A
teenage boy was working on an upturned bicycle in
front of the garage, two little girls of about ten were
sitting on the front doorstep with dolls on their laps and
a scatter of tiny dolls' clothes spread around them, a
boy of around seven was riding about on a tricycle and a
toddler of indeterminate sex was sitting in a sandpit,
banging an upturned bucket with a spade. It looked as
though Edna Pocock had more than made up for her
earlier misfortunes.

The little girls, absorbed in their game, did not
notice him until he was almost upon them and then
they looked up. They were so close in age that they
must either be friends or non-identical twins, Thanet
thought. One was as fair as the other was dark. The
dark one looked up unsmilingly at him as the fair one
jumped up, beaming.

"Hullo," he said. "Are your parents in?"

They exchanged a solemn look before the fair girl
nodded. "They're round the back," she said. "I'll show
you."

Thanet felt himself to be the focus of many eyes as
he followed his guide. The teenager had straightened
up, spanner in hand and the other boy had brought his
tricycle to a halt. Only the toddler remained oblivious
of the visitor, completely absorbed in his sand pies.
There was, Thanet felt, something wary, almost hostile

in this silent scrutiny. He smiled at the seven-year-old, raised his hand in a salute to the teenager, but neither responded. Thanet shrugged inwardly. If they didn't want to be friendly there was nothing he could do about it. He turned his attention to the girl beside him. As if aware of his discomfort she gave him an encouraging smile.

"What's your name?" he asked.

"Melanie. Melly for short."

Thanet did not believe in talking down to children. "What did I do wrong?" he said.

She glanced back over her shoulder, shrugged. "Nothing. It's not you, really. They're always like that."

Following her glance Thanet was slightly surprised to see that all four other children had now left what they were doing and were trailing behind, at a distance. Curiosity? He didn't know, but once again he had that curious impression of wariness, mistrust.

They were now about to turn the corner of the house into the back garden and Melly put up her hand. "Could you wait here a minute?" she said.

Thanet stopped, glanced back again. The other children had stopped too. Their solemn, watchful gaze reminded him very much of natives scrutinising the first white man to come their way. Of course, he thought, that was it. They were afraid. But why?

Before he could begin to think about this, however, Melly returned. "It's all right," she said. "Come on."

By now Thanet was intensely curious and he approached the small, sheltered terrace in the angle of the house with interest. After this build-up the two people who advanced to meet him seemed disappointingly nondescript. The man was of medium height with crinkled, greying hair, a drooping moustache and a solid, well-muscled frame. The woman was shorter than he and plump, with the tiny hands and feet of the type. She was wearing a shapeless dress in indeterminate colours and her plain features were not enhanced by untidy brown hair pulled back into a straggling bun. Not a woman who cared for appearances, Thanet thought.

Then, as she smiled in welcome he realised that she was not nondescript at all. The warmth of her personality was something very special indeed.

As he introduced himself the smile faded, however, and her eyes went beyond him to where the children stood silently watching, some yards away.

"It's . . . it's not anything to do with the kids?" she said anxiously.

Thanet was puzzled. "No, of course not. Why should it be?"

She sighed then, a tiny exhalation of relief, and raised her hand. "It's OK, kids, nothing to do with you," she called to them, and Thanet watched astonished as the little group erupted into noisy relief and ran, whooping and calling, back around the corner of the house.

Roger Pocock was setting up another folding deckchair and his wife waved Thanet into it. "They're not ours," she explained. "They're all foster kids and they're always scared stiff of being taken away. When anyone turns up unexpectedly they always think the worst. They've all had a bad time and they're used to being moved around from pillar to post at the drop of a hat."

"I see," Thanet said, and he did. He looked at Edna Pocock with new respect. "It must be very difficult work."

She smiled, that warm, transforming smile again. "Oh it is. But we enjoy it, don't we, Rodge?"

Her husband nodded and both men followed her gaze to the corner of the house, where the younger boy had just come into sight on his tricycle. "You wouldn't believe the difference it makes to them, once they settle down and begin to feel part of the family," she said. "Anyway," and she settled herself more comfortably in her chair, "you haven't come here to talk about them, so . . . ?"

They both looked at him with mild curiosity, the embodiment of people with easy consciences.

Thanet was feeling distinctly uncomfortable. The generosity of this couple made his enquiries seem almost obscene. How many people, he wondered, would be willing to fill their lives with the battered survivors of other people's tragic mistakes? Certainly no one could do so who did not genuinely love children and have their welfare at heart. No wonder those poor kids had treated his appearance with such suspicion. Nevertheless he was on a murder enquiry and questions had to be asked. He decided to be honest about how he felt.

"Look," he said, "I came here to ask some very unpleasant questions. Now that I've seen you, seen the children . . . well, frankly I find it difficult to put them."

"No need to feel like that," Edna Pocock said reassuringly. "It's nothing to do with the kids, you say, and I really can't think Rodge and me have done anything criminal, so go ahead. Ask away."

A crash, a scream, a rising crescendo of sobs interrupted the conversation. In a flash she was out of her chair, hurrying towards the corner of the house. There was a babble of raised voices and she returned, carrying the younger boy whose knee was bleeding badly. The other children trooped behind her, Melly leading the toddler by the hand.

"I'm sorry," Edna Pocock said. "I'll have to go in and see to this."

Thanet nodded his understanding and she went into the house, the other children following. If one of their number was threatened, it seemed, they habitually closed ranks, drawing comfort from proximity.

Roger Pocock caught Thanet's eye, shrugged. "They're good kids," he said. "Can we get your questions over while my wife's inside?"

If they did, Thanet guessed, Pocock would tell some white lies when she came back, to reassure her. Any why not? he asked himself. Wouldn't he try to protect Joan in the same way, in similar circumstances? He made up his mind. "It's about last Tuesday evening," he said. "I'm afraid I can't explain, but I would be grateful if you could tell me what you and your wife were doing."

Pocock frowned. "You're asking us for alibis?"

"In a way. It's just that there are some loose ends in a case I'm working on, and they've got to be tidied away. You and your wife might be able to help." It was lame, and he knew it. Pocock, he could tell, knew it too. He hoped the man wouldn't press for details.

Pocock looked at him in silence for a few moments, clearly debating whether or not to do so. Then he shrugged. "Well, I can't see that either of us was doing anything we shouldn't have been. My wife always goes to evening classes on Tuesday, and I babysit for her."

"And this was what happened last Tuesday?"

"Yes, I'm sure of it. She's never missed a class yet, unless she's ill or one of the children can't be left. She's doing pottery."

Thanet steeled himself and said, "Is there anyone who can vouch for either of you?"

Pocock's expression hardened. "My wife's classmates, I suppose. And the kids for me, if they have to. But I don't want them dragged into this if I can help it."

"No," Thanet said. And then, feeling a heel, "Is there any way we could do it without upsetting them?"

Pocock scowled. "I don't know. If we have to, I suppose."

The sound of voices announced that the others were returning.

"Leave it to me," Pocock said hurriedly.

The children all crowded around as the boy exhibited his bandaged knee. Edna Pocock sat down and flapped her hand at them. "Go on now," she said. "Off you go." She turned to Thanet as they began reluctantly to drift away. "This one hour on Sunday afternoons is the only time we keep for ourselves. It does them good, makes them think of someone else for a change."

Pocock had been watching the children thoughtfully and now he suddenly called after them. "Hey kids, come back a minute, will you?" He waited until they had come flocking back and then said, "Mr Thanet here and me have been having an argument. He says no one can ever remember properly what they were doing five days ago. Now I say you can. So let's see if we can prove him wrong, shall we?"

Four pairs of eyes swivelled to Thanet, one of them wary. Pocock's ploy had clearly not fooled the older boy. The toddler, of course, had not understood either the question or its significance. Seeing his opportunity for an unexpected cuddle he simply climbed up on to Edna's lap and burrowed his face into her ample breasts.

"Course we can," said Melly scornfully. Then, turning hesitantly to Pocock, "What day was that, Dad?"

"Tuesday," said Pocock, "Say Tuesday evening."

Edna Pocock glanced questioningly at her husband and he shook his head slightly in warning. Leave it, the gesture said.

The children were silent, thinking back.

"Aw, this is stupid," said the older boy suddenly. He took a pack of chewing gum from his pocket and distributed sticks as if they were reassurance. Then he leaned against the wall of the house, nonchalantly. "Course we can remember," he said deliberately, watching Thanet, challenging him. "Mum was at evening class and we were all here. Dad, Melly, Sally and me watched *The Pacemakers*."

"That's right, Dad, we did." It was Melly's turn now, her face alight with triumph. "Don't you remember, Dad? You said Sally and me could watch till nine so long as we promised that if we came to a bit you didn't think we ought to see we'd close our eyes. And there was that bit about the operation and you said don't look, and we didn't."

"I should hope not!" said Edna Pocock. "So that's what you get up to while I'm out, is it?" But she was not really angry, only pretending to be, as Thanet and the children could tell by her affectionate glance at Pocock. "All right, kids, that's enough now. I think we've proved your Dad's point. Off you go."

They went noisily this time, pleased at their triumphant refutal of Thanet's so-called theory.

Then she turned to Thanet. "And now," she said quietly, "perhaps you'd tell me what all this is about."

She listened in silence as Thanet explained in much the same terms as he had to her husband, then said, "Well, I was at evening class, like Rodge says. I left here about a quarter to seven, left the class as soon as it ended at nine and got back here about a quarter past."

"How did you go? By car? Bus?"

"By car."

So, Thanet thought with sinking heart, Edna Pocock could still be his quarry. "You can confirm that your wife arrived home around nine-fifteen?" he said.

Pocock nodded. "Around then. It was well before *The Pacemakers* ended, anyway."

And that was at nine-thirty. "You can't be more precise?"

"No I bloody well can't. And if you . . ." He glanced down at the restraining hand Edna put on his sleeve, took a deep breath and continued in a tight, hard voice, "If Edna says a quarter past nine, a quarter past nine it was."

He'd have to leave it there. Thanet heaved himself awkwardly out of his deck chair, apologised for disturbing their Sunday afternoon and left.

The interview had made him feel uncomfortable, guilty almost, and angry with himself for feeling so. At the traffic lights in the High Street he stalled his engine, grated a gear change. He swore.

There were times when he hated being a policeman.

14

By the time Thanet had finished the reports on the day's interviews he had had enough. He tidied his desk and headed for home, feeling in need of the comfort Joan's company would bring him.

Tomorrow there was much to be done. First he would send a team to make enquiries at Maddison House, to see if anyone could be found to confirm or disprove Alice Giddy's claim that she had spent Tuesday evening at home. Also, enquiries would have to be made at the Technical College. He would have to contact Edna Pocock's pottery teacher, check that she had indeed attended her class that evening and, if necessary, get a complete list of the members of the class and question them all, find out if any of them saw where she went when the session ended.

It certainly seemed that his five suspects had been reduced to two. Peake dead, Plummer in hospital, Pocock alibied by the children. Thanet believed them. He wouldn't have put it past the elder boy to lie on behalf of his foster father, but he certainly couldn't believe that Melly had done so. He was pretty certain she had been unaware of the significance of her contribution. No, when Julie was killed, Pocock had been sitting at home in front of the television set. Thanet only wished that the same could be said of his wife.

Was it possible that that kind, motherly woman could have killed twice? Reluctantly, he had to admit

that it was. It was common knowledge that in defence
of her children even the mildest of women could become a tigress and in Edna Pocock maternal love was
stronger than in most. If she had thought that Julie
could destroy the secure world that Edna and her
husband had so painstakingly built up for those children
... yes, Edna Pocock was still very much in the running.

As indeed was Alice Giddy. Now there was someone whom he could very well imagine a murderess.
Unlike Edna, who would kill from passion, Alice would
set about it in a cool and calculated manner, making
sure that the risks she took were minimal. There was no
doubt about it, of the two he very much hoped that she
would prove to be the guilty one.

It was quite wrong of him, of course, to hope
anything of the sort. His job was to see that justice was
done and if he didn't very much like what his investiga-
tions turned up, that was just too bad. For that matter,
even if he did find out which one of them was guilty, he
couldn't at the moment see how he was going to prove
it.

Thanet grimaced and pulled up behind an ice-
cream van parked at the side of the road. He'd buy
some choc ices to take home.

"Oh, lovely," said Joan, receiving the newspaper-
wrapped parcel with a kiss. "In the kitchen to eat these,
don't you think?"

Thanet watched Ben and Bridget as they ate the
ices. Most of Ben's seemed to end up on chin, hands or
bib, whereas Bridget approached hers fastidiously, taking neat, incisive bites and holding it carefully by the
wrapper. Thanet thought of the Pocock children earlier
in the afternoon, of their wariness and fear when a
stranger arrived. Sprig might feel shy, but never
threatened. She and Ben were secure in their little
world and please God they would stay that way. Once,
Julie Holmes must have felt just as safe in hers and
then, without warning, it had disintegrated. She had
lost father, home and confidence in other people in one
fell swoop. Thanet was convinced that, whoever the

murderer was, Julie had known her as a friend of her mother's. It was scarcely surprising that she had grown up wary, unable to commit herself to others for fear of being hurt. A wave of protective passion swept through him and he picked Sprig up, choc ice and all, and hugged her.

"Darling, look at your jacket!" Joan rinsed a cloth in cold water and began to sponge at the smear on his lapel. "What's the matter?" she said softly.

He shook his head, pulled a face. "Just this damned case." But he knew that he was telling only half the truth, that what was really upsetting him was the thought of the Pocock children. Damaged as they already were, how much more so would they be if Mrs Pocock proved to be the murderer? Was the case, which had begun so many years ago with another damaged child, Julie, to end by ruining more young lives? And was he to be the instrument of destruction?

Joan was chatting on now about something that had happened earlier in the day. He tried to concentrate. Someone, he gathered, had asked her to do something and she hadn't been able to say yes because of the children. And then this someone had made Joan feel thoroughly guilty, had implied that Joan had refused simply because she couldn't be bothered to help.

"Wretched woman!" Thanet said, indignant on Joan's behalf.

"But she made me feel so awful... honestly, people who haven't got children just don't seem to take them into account, don't realise how one has to arrange things around them, especially when they're little like... What's the matter?"

"What you said, just then. Say it again."

Joan repeated her complaint

Thanet stared at her, frowning. There was something in what she had said that was important for him, but he couldn't put his finger on it. What *was* it?

"Did I say something wrong?" Joan was looking puzzled. "Don't you agree with what I was saying?"

"What? Oh yes. Yes, of course, love. It's just that

I . . ." He shook his head. "It's no good. It won't come. Something you said rang a bell, but I can't think why."

Joan picked Ben up and began to wipe away the smears of chocolate. "You know what's the matter with your daddy?" she said to the baby. "He's been working too hard. There." She set Ben down on the floor again, handed him his favourite toy, a very noisy rattle, and came across to put her arm around Thanet's shoulders and drop a kiss on his forehead. "And you know my remedy for overwork? A nice quiet evening doing nothing. Watch television, listen to music, let your mind go blank, recuperate."

Thanet leaned his head against her breasts. "That's easier said than done, love."

"I know that, of course I do. But we can at least try."

So they did. But all through the evening Thanet was aware of a steadily increasing pressure at the back of his mind. Deliberately he held it a bay, wanting Joan to believe that her therapy was working, and it was not until they were in bed and her steady breathing told him that she was asleep, that he allowed himself at last to return to the question that had been niggling away at him all evening. What was it, in what Joan had said, that had been significant for him? He tried to recall her exact words. "People who haven't got children just don't seem to take them into account."

And then, seemingly out of nowhere, he heard Lineham's voice saying, "Why should anyone start to wonder whether the child had witnessed the murder?"

Only someone who did take children into account would have done so.

Thanet lay rigid, staring at the ceiling, willing himself not to disturb Joan by jumping out of bed and beginning to pace restlessly about the room

There was only one person who, twenty years ago, would have taken little Julie Parr into account, and that was Edna Pocock. She knew the Parrs, might well have babysat for them. Even then she had been, Inspector Low had said, a woman who loved children.

Thanet thought back, trying to project himself into her mind at the time of Annabel's murder. Edna Pocock had been expecting a child. She had already had more than one miscarriage and must have been hoping, passionately, that this time her pregnancy would go smoothly. Then she discovers that her husband is chasing Annabel. What if she had taken him to task about it? Suppose they had quarrelled, that Edna had become hysterical, that she had even flown at him and he, in defending himself, had struck back, causing her miscarriage? How would she have felt lying there in bed, her hopes shattered once again, full of bitterness and anger against her husband and against the woman who had been the cause of it all? Might she not had decided to confront Annabel, to tell her what she had done, to make her realise her responsibility for the death of Edna's unborn child?

Thanet could see it all: Edna, unhinged by grief, laying her plans, seizing the opportunity when it came; hurrying through the foggy night to Annabel's house, being admitted by the unsuspecting girl, following her up to the studio. Then would come the accusation. Annabel must have said or done something which snapped the last thread of Edna's control. Edna seizes the piece of quartz, strikes Annabel in a frenzy and then departs, unaware that all the time, in the half-curtained alcove at the far end of the room, Julie, rigid and silent with terror, has been watching.

Then would come the aftermath of the murder, the news of David Parr's death, of Jennifer having been the one to find Annabel's body. It would not have taken Edna long, with her child-orientated mind, to begin to wonder where Julie had been while her mother was at the hospital. Discreet enquiries might have led her to the inescapable conclusion that Jennifer had gone to the studio that night because Annabel had been looking after Julie, and Jennifer's hasty departure from the village would have confirmed what by now Edna might have suspected, that Julie might well have witnessed the murder.

She must have waited in terror at first for Julie to identify her. When it hadn't happened she must slowly have begun to recover her confidence, to think that even if Julie had been in Annabel's house, she couldn't have seen what had happened.

Years later, abandoning hope of having children of her own she must have conceived the plan of being a foster mother. Her husband, perhaps shocked out of his infidelities by the consequences of his pursuit of Annabel and anxious to make amends, must have fallen in with her plans. All had gone smoothly until the evening of the Private View. There Edna sees Julie, her mother's double, and wonders if Julie might have recognised her. She has to find out: did Julie witness the murder and if so, has she now recognised Edna as the murderer? All the old terrors of discovery are reawakened. Now she has far more to lose and she cannot afford to indulge in foolish optimism. She must find out for sure.

So as not to arouse her husband's suspicions Edna decides to go and see Julie on her pottery class evening, Tuesday. But first she has to find out Julie's address. This might not have been easy and would perhaps account for the lapse of a fortnight between the evening of the Private View and Julie's murder. She goes to Gladstone Road, finds Julie hysterical after the quarrel with Kendon. There is a struggle and Julie is stabbed. Edna runs, the pattern having repeated itself. On neither occasion did she set out with murder in mind, on each circumstances combined to cause her to commit it.

A lot of this was speculation again, of course, nevertheless it fitted, in its broad outline, with all the known facts.

Except... Thanet scowled up at the ceiling, shifted restlessly. Joan turned over, murmured something in her sleep and he froze, keeping quite still until the even pattern of her breathing had been re-established.

Except that the time element did not fit.

If his story was true, Kendon had left Julie between eight-forty and eight-forty-five. If night school had not ended until nine, it would have been at least

ten or a quarter past by the time Edna arrived, having
parked her car somewhere out of sight (two points to
check up on: what make of car did she drive, had
anyone in the Gladstone Road area seen it that night?).
By then Julie would surely have calmed down, have
taken her coat off and put that carving knife away?

Unless Edna had left her class early? A pottery
class was not like an academic session. People would be
moving about all the time, working to different schedules.
If Edna had made sure that she finished early on
Tuesday, had left before the class ended . . . ? More
checking.

And, at the end of it, no real satisfaction, if he
were proved right. Those children . . .

Thanet spent a restless night.

15

Thanet arrived at the office next day with none of the eager anticipation he usually felt at this stage of an enquiry. His quarry might be in sight, but the hunt had lost its savour. He saw no joy whatsoever in the prospect of tracking down Edna Pocock.

First, however, he had to determine whether or not Alice Giddy could definitely be eliminated as a suspect and he turned to the batch of reports which Baker had written on his enquiries at Maddison House in connection with Parrish. In the hours before dawn Thanet had had a faint recollection of something that he had read in one of them. . . .

At this point Lineham walked in.

"What the hell are you doing here?" said Thanet.

Lineham looked terrible, like a rag doll whose stuffing had gone limp.

"Home," said Thanet, crossing the room, taking him by the shoulders and propelling him firmly towards the door. "Bed. And I don't want to see you again until you're properly fit."

"But, sir. . . ."

"Home," repeated Thanet. "What are you trying to do, start a flu epidemic? In any case, what use do you think you'd be here, in that state?" Seeing Lineham's face, Thanet relented. "Oh look, Mike, I know how you feel, having to duck out at this stage, but you really have no choice, have you? Have you seen a doctor?"

"Not yet, no."

161

"In case he told you not to come back to work, I suppose. Well, call him. You'll be back all the sooner if you get proper treatment."

When Lineham had made his reluctant exit Thanet returned to the sheaf of reports on Maddison House. Of course, when Baker had been sent out there he had simply been concerned to find out whether or not anyone had seen Parrish either entering or leaving the building on the evening of the murder. All the same, Thanet was sure . . . Ah yes, here it was.

Mrs Barret of Flat 27 had not seen or heard anything relevant to Baker's enquiry as she had spent the evening watching television first of all at home and then in the flat of a neighbour.

There had been four doors on Alice Giddy's landing, Thanet remembered. Hers, Flat 26, had been the second from the left. She should, then, be Mrs Barret's next-door neighbour. Baker reported that the occupants of Flats 26 and 28 had been out when he called. Presumably he had not returned to them later because he had been called off the enquiry before he could do so; when Phyllis Penge, Parrish's mistress, had confirmed Parrish's alibi, Thanet had not considered further enquiries necessary.

So, which neighbour had Mrs Barret spent the evening with? Alice Giddy or the occupant of Flat 28?

Thanet picked up the telephone. "D.C. Baker in?"

Baker, he learned, had just gone out, would not be back until late morning.

Thanet swore under his breath. "Send him up the minute he gets back, will you?"

He could either ring or go to see Mrs Barret himself, but he would prefer to talk to Baker first. He didn't want to risk alerting Alice Giddy any further until he was more sure of his ground. He would wait.

Glancing at his watch he saw that by now the Administrative Staff should have arrived at the Technical College. He checked the telephone number and dialled.

Edna Pocock's pottery teacher, a Mrs Caroly, apparently worked at the College on only two evenings a week. The secretary had no idea whether Mrs Caroly had a day-time job. There was an address and telephone number, however, and she gave them to Thanet. She could supply a list of the names and addresses of the class members and Thanet arranged that someone would call around to pick it up within the next half an hour.

He sent Carson off on this errand, then tried Mrs Caroly's number. There was no reply. Another man was despatched to find out where she was and when she would be available.

Now what? Thanet rang through for some coffee, stood up and moved restlessly across to the window. Outside lay the promise of another beautiful spring day. A breeze had sprung up and fluffy white clouds promenaded across the sky. The traffic had thinned now that the morning rush was over, and the people on the streets were moving in a more leisurely manner: young mothers with a pram and a toddler in tow, old men with no object but to find somewhere warm and quiet where they might pass the dragging hours. Watching one of them Thanet was invaded by melancholy. Is that where life led? Was that how he would end up, thirty years from now?

A young constable arrived bearing Thanet's coffee.

Thanet turned away from the window, sat down again. The coffee was lukewarm and he grimaced in disgust.

A knock at the door and Mallard came in. "My," he said, "aren't we cheerful this morning!"

"Hullo Doc," Thanet said. "Want some coffee?"

"If that's a specimen of what'll be produced if I say yes," said Mallard peering into Thanet's cup, "then no, thank you. I have too much respect for my digestive system."

"I think we can do better than this," Thanet said, picking up the telephone.

"How's the back?" Mallard asked, while they waited for fresh coffee.

"Oh, much better, thanks. I hardly think of it now."

"Good."

The coffee, when it came, was hot and strong. As they sipped in silence Thanet became increasingly uncomfortable under Mallard's scrutiny. Consciously he avoided meeting his eye.

"Well," Mallard said at last, putting his cup down with a gesture of finality, "if you won't tell me, I'll have to ask, though I'm damned if I see why I should. If your back's all right, what's the matter? Case going badly?"

Thanet shrugged. "It's going," he said. "Which is more than could be said a few days ago."

"Then why the long face?"

Thanet looked away, out of the window. High up an aeroplane glinted silver. Some lucky devils off somewhere, he thought irrelevantly. "I just don't like the way it's going, that's all."

Mallard studied him in silence for a moment or two longer, then leaned forward. "Correct me if I'm wrong, but do I understand you to say that although you're making progress in the investigation, you are unhappy about it?"

"That's right."

"Why? Because you think you are investigating along the wrong lines, or because you don't like what you're finding out?"

"The latter, I suppose."

"Well well. So you don't like what you're finding out," Mallard said sarcastically. "How d'you think I'd go on working at all, if I allowed myself to feel like that?" He heaved himself out of his chair, stumped across to the window. "I'll tell you this, Luke. If I allowed all those corpses to be anything more than specimens to me, I'd go mad at the sheer bloody waste of it all." He spun around, pointed a finger at Thanet. "And as you know perfectly well, that's how it should be with you. The minute you let yourself get involved, you're sunk, finished, kaput." He returned to his chair, plumped down in it. "So don't you forget it," he said.

He was right, of course, Thanet thought. And

yet . . . it was so much easier for Mallard. He dealt only with the dead.

"Oh, I know what you're thinking," Mallard said disconcertingly. "You're thinking it's easier to switch off when you're dealing with corpses. And you're right, of course. It is to a certain extent, anyway. But just remember this: you are not here to judge, just to investigate. So don't try taking over the Almighty's job. He's much better at it than you could ever be." He glanced at his watch. "I'll have to go now." He stood up. "It is the Holmes case we've been talking about?"

Thanet nodded.

"I don't know what right I have to go sounding off at you like this. If it'll make you feel any better, the truth of the matter is that it's myself I'm angry with, really, for being in the same boat. I've just been doing a P.M. on a child. She was only five . . . It's a hell of a life sometimes, isn't it?"

He and Thanet exchanged a rueful grin before Mallard went out, closing the door behind him with uncharacteristic gentleness.

Thanet looked after him, thoughtfully, and then picked up the telephone. Mallard was right. He had been becoming positively maudlin. "If Carson's back, send him in."

Thanet took the proffered list of Edna Pocock's classmates and studied it. There were twelve names in all. Quickly he ran his finger down them, noting the addresses, then returned to the second name on the page. Mrs A. Bligh, 14 Upper Mole Road. He reached for his town map and checked. Yes, as he thought, this was the next turning off the Canterbury Road beyond Little Mole Road. If Mrs Bligh travelled by car, she would no doubt take the same route home as Edna Pocock. . . .

He made up his mind. Not a telephone call this time. He would go and visit Mrs Bligh himself.

Mrs Bligh was short, plump and thirtyish with a frizz of tightly permed blond hair. She was wearing a flowing smock dress in shrieking greens and orange which merely served to accentuate her generous curves. Her reaction, like that of most people who are unexpectedly faced with a CID man on the doorstep, was puzzled, apprehensive and somewhat wary. She studied his warrant card carefully before inviting him in.

"We'll have to go into the kitchen, Inspector. My little girl's in there."

In this house Monday was still washing day, Thanet saw as he followed her into a large, light kitchen, well-equipped with mod. cons. A long central table was covered with piles of washing, some dry, some wet, and an automatic washing machine was making an infernal row in one corner.

"Just a minute, I'll switch it off," shouted Mrs Bligh.

The resulting silence was almost deafening. "It makes an awful din," she said apologetically, as if she were personally responsible for the machine's noisiness, "but it saves so much work I try not to notice it. Sandra, this is Mr Thanet."

Sandra was about the same age as Bridget. She was standing on a chair at the kitchen sink, arms plunged into a froth of bubbles.

"Hullo, Sandra," Thanet said. "My little girl likes doing that, too."

Mrs Bligh, apparently reassured by this evidence of Thanet's humanity, gave a timid smile. "Sit down, Inspector, won't you?" She pulled out a chair at the long table, pushed aside a pile of clothes. "Sorry about the mess," she murmured, seating herself opposite him.

"That's quite all right," Thanet said dismissively. "Now then, I expect you're wondering why I've called. There's nothing to worry about, I assure you. There was an incident last Tuesday evening and we're trying to trace witnesses."

"What sort of incident?" Mrs Bligh said nervously.

"Don't worry," Thanet said gently. "There really is

no need. Now I understand that on Tuesday evenings you attend a pottery class at the Technical College."

"Yes. But how did you . . . ?"

"I'm sorry, but I really can't give you any more information. Please, Mrs Bligh, just relax. If you can't help us, I'll go away and we'll forget all about it."

She did relax a little now, sat back in her chair.

"You attended the class last Tuesday?"

"Yes."

"And stayed the full length of time?"

"Yes."

"So you left at nine, as usual?"

"That's right."

"And you came home by your usual route—I'm sorry, I forgot to ask. Do you go by car?"

"Yes. I do. And yes, I came home by the same route as usual last week."

"That would be right at the entrance to the Technical College, left into Wallace way . . . ?"

"Yes. Then let me see . . ." she gave a nervous laugh. "I do it so often it's automatic. Yes, then left into Park Road, left again into Canterbury Road, then straight on all the way until I turn into this road."

"Good. Now, I want you to think very carefully. On your way along Canterbury Road last Tuesday evening, did you see anything unusual?" The question, of course, was misleading. To his knowledge Canterbury Road had been as peaceful and well-ordered as Sunday Morning Service last Tuesday, but he wanted to divert Mrs Bligh's attention from the real purpose of his visit.

"No, I don't think so. Let me think." Her eyes narrowed in concentration as she searched her memory. "No, I'm sure I didn't."

"Right, thank you." Thanet stood up. "You don't happen to know of anyone else who regularly travels by that route on Tuesday evenings, do you?"

"Well, there's Mrs Pocock, she lives in Little Mole Road. She comes to the same class as me."

"You travel together, you mean?"

"Oh no. My husband works in London, you see,

and I'm never quite sure what time he's going to get home, so it's awkward to travel with anyone else. I mean, it's bad enough having to be late yourself, but if you make other people late as well . . ."

"Yes, of course. But Mrs Pocock? She attended class last Tuesday?"

"Yes. She works next to me, as a matter of fact. We're both learning the same technique at the moment, and we tend to compare notes a lot."

"And she comes home by the same route as you?" Thanet's palms were beginning to sweat as he approached the crucial question.

"Yes. It's the most direct way, of course."

"And last Tuesday. Do you happen to remember if she left before you?"

"No, we left together. In fact, I followed her car all the way home from the Tech. I remember thinking how clean hers was, in comparison with ours, and deciding I really must get my husband to wash it at the weekend."

"You followed her all the way home," echoed Thanet flatly.

She misread his incredulity as disappointment. "Yes, I'm sorry. So that means she wouldn't have seen anything either—not unless it's just that I'm completely unobservant and missed noticing something she might have seen."

"You're absolutely certain you were behind her all the way?"

"Yes, I told you, her car . . ."

"I see," said Thanet with finality. "Well, thank you very much, Mrs Bligh. I'm sorry to have taken up so much of your time." At the front door he paused. "I forgot to ask. What time do you usually get home on Tuesday evenings?"

"At about a quarter past nine, give or take a minute or two."

"And last Tuesday?"

She shrugged. "Same as usual, I suppose. I didn't really notice. But I wasn't held up at all, so it must have been about then."

Thanet reiterated his thanks and left.

He drove around the corner and parked. He felt dazed, disorientated. So, he had been wrong about Edna Pocock. That was a relief, but a frustration too. That moment of illumination last night had been a sham, the hours of agonising over her foster children a total waste of time and emotional energy. What a fool he had been!

He put the car savagely into gear and was half way back to the office before fear began to niggle away at him. Out of the original five suspects only Alice Giddy was now left. If her alibi for the night of Julie's murder proved as watertight as Edna Pocock's, if she too were innocent . . . Thanet shook his head, a tight, angry little shake. No, it wasn't possible. For in that case his whole beautiful theory would collapse around him like a house of cards. There would be no double murderer and the Dacre painting, The Private View, the fact that Julie had witnessed a murder as a child, none of this would have any relevance to his case.

He would be back where he started, days ago.

Back at the station the constable on duty raised a startled face at Thanet's snapped "Baker back yet?" Thanet was not usually so peremptory.

"Yes sir. Gone up to the canteen, sir."

"Find him," Thanet said. "Now. And send him up to my office."

The man was already reaching for the phone. "Right away, sir."

Thanet paced restlessly up and down while he waited. No, he couldn't, wouldn't believe it. All that patient, painstaking unravelling of past and present, the beautiful logic, the *rightness* of it all . . .

"Sir?"

News of Thanet's mood must have travelled. Baker looked distinctly apprehensive. Thanet experienced a pang of compunction. Why should Baker be put through the mill just because he, Thanet, was furious with himself?

"It's all right, Baker," he said, with an attempt at a

smile. "You haven't done anything wrong. I just need your help, that's all." He sat down, shuffled through the papers on his desk, selected the one he wanted. "It's to do with those enquiries you made at Maddison House, in connection with Parrish's alibi for the night of the Holmes murder. Now, in your report you state that a Mrs Barret of Flat 27 spent part of the evening watching television with a neighbour. Do you happen to know which neighbour?"

Baker had already taken out his notebook and was leafing through it. "Ah yes, I remember her," he said, as he searched. "Couldn't stop talking. Her set broke down just after *The Pacemakers* started, and her son's a fan, wouldn't give her any peace until she went to ask if they could watch next door. Ah, here it is. They went to Flat 26, occupied by Alice Giddy. I didn't actually interview Miss Giddy, sir. She . . ."

"Was out, I know. Then you were pulled off the enquiries because they were no longer considered necessary." Thanet was doing his best to ignore the sinking feeling in the pit of his stomach. "They stayed until the end of the programme?"

"Yes, sir."

"Did she by any chance say anything to indicate that Miss Giddy was actually there with them all the time, watching the programme?"

Baker consulted his notes, considered. "Not specifically, no, sir. But by implication, yes. I mean, like I said, the woman went on and on and on. I mean, I heard all about Miss Giddy, how stand-offish she is and how she—Mrs Barret, I mean—wouldn't have plucked up the courage to ask if it hadn't been for her son going on and on about it. And how Miss Giddy was a *Pacemakers* fan herself and that Mrs Barret had therefore felt that it might be all right to ask her after all as Miss Giddy would know how she would have felt if her set had gone wrong just after the programme started. I really think she would have mentioned it if after all this Miss Giddy had gone out at all during the programme."

"So you really don't think she could have slipped

out for, say, twenty minutes or so?" The absolute minimum time necessary to get from Maddison House to Gladstone Road and back again, Thanet considered.

"No sir, I don't. Honestly, if you'd heard the way she goes on . . . she just isn't the sort to keep anything back."

"Intelligent?"

"Not particularly."

"Do you think you could find out from her whether Miss Giddy did in fact go out at all during *The Pacemakers* without arousing her suspicions?"

"I should think so, sir."

"Good. Do it now. Oh Baker . . ."

"Yes sir?" Baker, already on his way to the door, turned back.

"I suppose there's no doubt in your mind that the woman's story was genuine?"

"About the set breaking down and going next door to watch? No, no doubt at all, sir. Her son was home when I called—he was off school for a dental appointment and from time to time she dragged him into the conversation—you know the sort of thing, 'Didn't we, Desmond, wasn't it, Desmond,' that sort of thing. I honestly don't think he was lying, just rather bored with the way she was going on and a bit embarrassed, as kids are at the age. He's about thirteen, I'd say. And apart from that, the repair engineer had just finished working on the set when I arrived. He was leaving as I came in."

"Which firm, did you notice?"

Baker screwed up his face in concentration. "I'm not sure. He was wearing an orange overall, I do remember that."

"White lettering?"

"I think so."

"Rentaset," Thanet said. He used the firm himself. "All right, thanks. Go and check now with Mrs Barret."

When Baker had gone, Thanet consulted the telephone directory. Until all this was confirmed he wouldn't allow himself to think . . .

It took only a few minutes for Rentaset to check their records and come back with the information that Mrs Barret had left a message on the Ansaphone at 8.35 pm on Tuesday May 6, and that the set had been repaired the following morning.

A few minutes later Baker returned. Alice Giddy had watched the entire programme with Mrs Barret and her son. So that really was the end of that particular road. Thanet thanked Baker, sent him off and then began to pace restlessly about the room.

He was a fool, a blind, self-opinionated fool.

After a while the confusion of anger and self-disgust in his mind settled down into a steady ache of disillusionment. Where had he gone wrong?

He sat down again, leaned back in his chair and, staring into space, began to work it out. Eventually, after a great deal of heart-searching, he came to the conclusion that he had been led astray by two factors: curiosity and vanity. Julie Holmes had intrigued him. He had wanted to understand her, to know what made her tick. The trail had led back into the past and he had followed it like a hound on the scent of the fox, deaf and blind to all else.

And vanity . . . oh yes, there was that, too. Hadn't he been delighted with his own cleverness in working out this elaborate double murder theory? The truth of the matter was that he was just plain incompetent. Even Lineham had seen it. What had he called Thanet's idea? Far-fetched, that was it. Far-fetched.

Thanet made a little *moue* of self-disgust as he remembered how outraged he had felt at Lineham's attitude, how he had pretended to take Lineham's objections seriously when all the while he was mentally discounting them.

There was something else that Lineham had said, too. What was it? "Isn't it much more likely that Julie Holmes was killed by someone involved with her now, in the present?"

But of course he, Thanet, in love with his theory,

had refused to listen. Well he would eat humble pie. He at least owed Lineham that.

Meanwhile . . . meanwhile he would have to begin all over again.

16

This time, Thanet swore, he would do things the right way around: facts first, theories afterwards. He began yet again to work systematically through every single report or statement which had been made or taken since the beginning of the case. Anger and self-disgust, he discovered, were wonderful aids to concentration but did not necessarily produce results. He found nothing significant which he had missed before, came across nothing which in any way shed new light on the problem.

What he did realise was that since setting off like a crazy, blind fool to prove his own cleverness, he had neglected to tie up one or two loose ends which now dangled reproachfully at him. Take the girl Kendon claimed to have seen, for example. Further efforts must be made to trace her. So far house-to-house enquiries had produced nothing, and there had been no response to the radio, television and newspaper appeals. Why?

There seemed to be three possible explanations: one, the girl did not listen to the radio, never watched television or read a newspaper—unlikely unless she had been out of the country or on holiday, perhaps. Thanet made a note: if necessary the appeals would be repeated at weekly intervals for the next three weeks.

Two, the girl did not exist. If she did not turn up in the next three weeks Thanet would presume that this was why, and devise a line of attack on Kendon.

Three, the girl existed, was aware that the police wished to see her, but did not want to come forward for some reason of her own—perhaps she didn't like the idea of her husband or family knowing where she was that night. Thanet made another note: make sure that the wording of the appeal be altered to make it clear that the police would treat information received from this witness as confidential as far as possible.

Meanwhile he would arrange that tomorrow evening, Tuesday, exactly one week from the murder, someone would be on duty at the railway station to question regular travellers. The ticket clerk had proved useless, a surly little man so uninterested in his customers that he didn't even bother to look up as he pushed the tickets across. Yet another note: question Kendon again about other people on the station that evening.

As far as Parrish was concerned there was one really glaring omission . . .

Thanet picked up the telephone again. "Send Bentley in, will you?"

News of Thanet's mood had clearly travelled. Bentley stood stiffly correct, avoiding Thanet's eye.

"It's all right," Thanet said, able now to be amused. "You can relax. I'm not going to bite this time."

Bentley's mouth twitched at one corner and his shoulders visibly relaxed.

"This man Horrocks, the salesman. I believe you questioned his wife, is that right?"

"Yes, sir."

"And I understand he was due back from his sales trip last night?"

"So she said, sir."

"Right, I want you to find out where he is and go and see him. Let's hope he hasn't flitted off again."

"His firm said he'd be in this area for three weeks after coming back, sir."

"Good. Now this really is very important. Horrocks first noticed Parrish's car parked in front of the shop at seven-fifteen. We know from Carne—that's the chap who was picking up his daughter from a music lesson—that it was still there at eight-twenty. Mrs Horrocks says that her husband left on his business trip just before nine, but that she doesn't know whether or not the Triumph was gone by then. The point is that Parrish claims that he was with his mistress from about ten past seven to nine-thirty. She confirms this and if it's true, of course, he's in the clear. But she may well be lying to protect him and I want to go and see her again. But first I want you to find out from Horrocks whether or not the Triumph was still there when he left just before nine."

"Right, sir."

I must be missing Lineham, Thanet thought as Bentley left. He didn't usually give long explanations when sending his men out on such simple errands. He stretched, then stood up. Suddenly he felt lethargic, stupefied, almost. The atmosphere in the room, he realised, was so thick with pipe smoke one could almost cut it into cubes. From his favourite position at the window the world outside beckoned to him, fresh and enticing. He glanced at his watch. He had completely missed his lunch-hour and could with justification take some time off. He had promised Joan that he would at some point try to get out to buy the Snoopy for which Sprig was yearning as a birthday present. In any case, his brain felt so addled that if he didn't have a break he might as well go home, for all the work he would be able to do.

He left his window open to freshen the room and set off down the High Street. It was good to feel part of the normal world again, to be an ordinary person going shopping for a birthday present for his small daughter. The purchase did not take long. Sprig's needs had been clearly defined. Thanet accepted the large, squashy parcel and wandered around the toy shop for a while before leaving. What a marvellous selection of toys there was for children these days! Surely toy shops had never been like this when he was young? He hung yearningly for some time over a complex model railway lay-out. Perhaps when Ben was older...

By the time he left he felt refreshed, with a pleasant sense of duty done. The office smelt sweeter now and Thanet balanced his large parcel on top of the

coat rack, so that he would see it without fail when he
went home, and sat down at his desk.

What now?

He tried without success to get hold of Kendon.
He would have to ring again this evening. Then he sat
staring at the pile of papers before him, drumming
impatient fingers on his desk. Surely Bentley should be
back soon? And if Horrocks confirmed that Parrish's car
had still been there at nine? More house-to-house
enquiries, he supposed, this time directed exclusively
towards finding out if anyone else had seen the Triumph
that night, noticed when it left.

Meanwhile there didn't seem to be a single thing
he could do.

What about Holmes? Should he perhaps try a
reconstruction of the crime, aimed at discovering whether or not Holmes could have committed the murder in
those fifteen or twenty seconds that had elapsed between the moment when he and Byfleet parted at the
front gate and the moment when Holmes had called
Byfleet back?

But all Thanet's original objections to the idea that
Holmes was the murderer still held. No, a reconstruction would be time-consuming and pointless.

It was possible, of course, that both Parrish and
Kendon were innocent too, that some casual caller or
potential burglar had been unlucky enough to have
happened to approach the house in Gladstone Road just
after Kendon's departure. Thanet groaned at the thought.
If that were so, unless some new evidence turned up of
its own accord, it looked as though the chances of
catching the murderer were very slim indeed, if not
non-existent. And to have to admit failure, particularly
in view of his own misguided behaviour . . .

A knock at the door, and Bentley entered. Thanet
could see at once that he had found something. Could it
be a break, at last?

It was. Horrocks, leaving his house at just before
nine o'clock and having to walk to his car, parked two
streets away, had been infuriated to find that he was

just in time to see the tail lights of the Triumph disappearing up the road.

"He's certain?" Thanet asked eagerly.

"Absolutely, sir. He'd been out every quarter of an hour or so all evening, as you know, so he really was mad just to have missed him like that."

"Good. Excellent. Well done, Bentley."

So Parrish had lied again. Thanet's immediate impulse was to confront the man, but instinct told him to go carefully indeed. Parrish was a very smooth customer. He would no doubt have prepared some tale in case of this very eventuality. Besides, Thanet would like to have some further confirmation of Horrocks's story. If Parrish had lied, so had his mistress.

Yes, a visit to Phyllis Penge was definitely the next priority.

Palmerston Row was noisy with the sound of children playing and Thanet prudently drove past, parked his car in front of Dobson's yard in Gladstone Road and walked back. The girl who answered the door of number 14 was younger than Thanet had expected, not much more than nineteen, he guessed. She had long, elaborately curled blonde hair, heavy eye make-up and wore a pink satin blouse and a tight black skirt slit to the knee on one side. Her welcoming smile slipped a little as Thanet introduced himself, and her eyes slid past him as if assessing the effect of his visit upon the neighbours.

"You'd better come in," she said, standing back.

Thanet had to squeeze past her in the narrow hall, and he was aware of the slither of satin against his sleeve, of a whiff of surprisingly good perfume before she pointed at a half-open door.

"In there," she said.

The room was comfortable, if claustrophobically full. Thanet's eyes skimmed over a three-piece suite, three strategically-placed coffee tables, a large glass-fronted drinks cabinet well stocked with bottles, an imposing stereo system, an elaborate radio-cassette, a long rack of records and another of cassettes, and one of the largest colour television sets Thanet had ever seen. There was not a book or a newspaper in sight.

She waved him into a chair and perched on the edge of the settee, tugging her skirt down over the knees as if conscious that too much exposed flesh was not appropriate to the occasion.

Thanet wondered if a formal approach might work best. The girl was obviously nervous—as well she might be, having lied to the police—and, he judged, ready to talk. If she had only told the truth when questioned last time Thanet might, he realised ruefully, have been saved from making a fool of himself. He couldn't feel angry with Lineham, though. Looking at the girl he now understood why Lineham had slipped up. Astute though the sergeant was, girls, especially sexually attractive girls like this, tended to throw him. Thanet found the thought comforting. After his own fiasco it was good to know that Lineham, too, had his Achilles heel.

"Now then, Mrs Penge," he said, taking a notebook from his pocket, flipping it open and pretending to consult it, "on Wednesday May 7 you made a statement to my sergeant regarding your movements on the evening of Tuesday May 6. Have you anything to add to that statement?"

She passed her tongue nervously over her lips. "What do you mean?"

"Would you like to alter or amend that statement in any way?"

A slight shake of the head. "I don't think so."

"Perhaps you'd like me to remind you of what you said in it? You state that on Tuesday May 6 you left this house at seven pm, walked along the footpath at the end of the cul-de-sac and entered the side door of a flat which is situated over the greengrocer's shop in Jubilee Street. This flat belongs to Mr Jeremy Parrish. He was waiting for you and you stayed with him until nine-thirty when you left. You then returned home."

He glanced at her. She was staring at him as if mesmerised, gnawing at the quick of her little finger.

"Well, Mrs Penge?"

She lowered her hand from her mouth, tugged again at the hem of her skirt, a jerky, nervous movement. "Well what?" she said, with an attempt at a coquettish smile.

"Your statement." Thanet tapped his notebook. "We just want to check that it is correct. So often, you see, people get flustered when they are asked to make a statement, and can't think straight. And then later on, when they've had a chance to think it over, they realise they got something wrong. Now I have a feeling that this happened in your case. Am I right?" There, he had given her a way to back down without losing face or being too afraid to admit it. Would she take it?

She shook her head slightly, a nervous, ambiguous movement.

He leaned forward, spoke very gently, reassuringly. "Please, Mrs Penge, it really is very important that we should know." And then, as she still said nothing, "Murder is a very serious business."

Her eyes dilated. "You're not saying . . . You don't mean Jeremy . . . ?"

"I'm not accusing anybody, Mrs Penge. But we have to know the truth, not just from some people but from everybody. That way we can slowly build up a picture of what happened on the night Mrs Holmes was killed. Did you know her?"

A quick, tight shake of the head.

Somehow he had to break through the barrier of her loyalty to Parrish. "She wasn't much older than you, you know. Just a young girl, with all her life before her." That was laying it on a bit thick, he knew, but it worked. Phyllis's identification with Julie lasted just long enough for her to burst out, "He said he'd tell. . ." and stop, knuckles pressed hard against her mouth, as if to hold the words in by force.

Thanet understood at once. "Mr Parrish said he'd tell your husband about his relationship with you, if you didn't back him up?" So it hadn't been loyalty which had held her back, but fear. The bastard. The out and out bastard.

She nodded and, burying her face in her hands, began to cry. It was a near-silent weeping, almost a mourning, Thanet thought as he thrust a clean handkerchief into her hand. For the death of love? he wondered, for illusions destroyed? Or was her reaction one of simple fear that now her husband would find out that she had been unfaithful?

"Now, I think you'd better tell me all about it, don't you? Mr Parrish said he'd tell your husband about your affair if you didn't back him up. Back him up over what?" He knew the answer, of course, but it was sweet to hear her say it.

"Over the time he said we'd stayed together until, that Tuesday evening," she said ungrammatically.

"Half past nine, you mean?" Then, as she nodded, he said softly, "So what time did you part?"

"Twenty-five to," she said, almost inaudibly.

"Twenty-five to nine?"

She nodded,

"You left together?"

"No. I always leave first. Jeremy stays behind to lock up and that."

"And you're sure about the time?"

"Certain sure." Her voice was stronger now. "There was something I specially wanted to see on the telly at nine so when I got down to the street I looked at my watch to see if there was time to nip along and pick up some chips before going home. I was hungry."

Thanet's stomach contracted with excitement. "The fish and chip shop in Jubilee Road?"

"Yes."

"And did you go?"

She nodded. "There was bags of time." Her eyes flickered away from his.

"You saw something, didn't you?" he said softly. "While you were in the shop?"

That startled her. "How did you . . . ?" She broke off, twisting his handkerchief nervously, looking miserably down at it as if it could give her guidance.

"How did I know that you saw Mr Parrish go by?" Her silence confirmed that he had guessed correctly. "Did he notice you?"

An almost imperceptible shake of the head.

"You were in the shop. . . ." he encouraged.

She relinquished the handkerchief as she came to her decision. "I saw him in the mirror," she said. "It's a big one, on the wall behind the counter. Ted—that's the chap what serves there—he bent down to pick something up and in the mirror, in the space where he'd been standing, like, I saw Jeremy go by. At first I thought, he's going to his car. But then I knew he couldn't be. It was parked between the flat and the chip shop, so he'd already passed it."

Thanet hazarded another guess. "So you went to the door, to see where he was going?"

She nodded.

"And?"

"He walked to the end of the road and turned . . . and turned left."

In the direction of Gladstone Road. "You're sure?"

"Yeah." She leaned her head against the back of the settee. The strain of the last few minutes was telling on her now.

"Thank you." He tucked his notebook in his pocket. "Just one other point, Mrs Penge. When, exactly, did Mr Parrish contact you and ask you to back up his false statement about the time he left?"

She thought for a moment. "In the afternoon, before your sergeant came to see me. He rang me at work."

After the second visit to Parrish, Thanet thought. He must have been on the phone to Phyllis the minute they left.

"Good," he said briskly. He rose. "Well now, if you'll come along with me to make a statement . . ."

She shrank back against the settee. "You're arresting me?" she whispered.

Thanet laughed. "No. No, of course not. All I want is a statement." And the certainty that as soon as he had left she wouldn't be on the phone to Parrish to warn him that the game was up. He didn't think she would but he had no intention of risking it. "All you have to do is tell one of my men exactly what you've been telling me, then he'll type it all for you, you'll read through what he's written to check that he's got it right, and you'll sign it. And that will be that, you'll be able to come home."

"Does . . . Will my husband have to know?"

"I'm sorry. I really can't say at the moment. It depends on what happens."

She looked so miserable that Thanet couldn't help feeling sorry for her. She was, after all, very young.

"Come on," he said gently. "We'd better be on our way."

17

────·──■■──■──■■──·──■■──·──■■──·────

It was five o'clock by the time Thanet arrived back at the police station. He handed Phyllis Penge over to Carson and told him to take her statement.

"Spin it out, will you? Don't let her make any phone calls and don't let her go until I say so. I've got to go out again."

Then he ran upstairs to his office, taking the steps two at a time. All the way back from Palmerston Row he had been trying to work out the best way to approach Parrish. It could now be proved that Parrish had been lying, but Thanet was well aware that there was still no shred of evidence to tie him in with the murder. Parrish could simply say that he had wanted a breath of fresh air after leaving the flat, had gone for a short stroll before returning to his car and driving off just before nine. He could claim that he had not dared tell the police this before, because he had been afraid that they wouldn't believe him.

And let's face it, Thanet thought, it might well be true. Parrish might yet be innocent—as innocent as Edna Pocock had proved to be. Thanet found himself reserving judgement. Once bitten, twice shy.

Just as he was parking his car, however, Thanet had had a stroke of inspiration, had suddenly seen a way in which he might, if he were very lucky, trap Parrish into an admission, if he were guilty. It might not work of course, such ploys frequently did not, but in this case there was just a chance and he was determined to take it. For it to work, however, his interview with Parrish—and he would take Bentley as a witness—would have to take place in Parrish's office, and preferably today. Thanet grabbed the telephone.

"Bentley? Bring Julie Holmes's effects up, will you? And fast, man."

Bentley arrived minutes later, out of breath. Thanet ignored the polythene bag in which Julie's clothes were shrouded and seized the large brown envelope in which smaller items had been placed. He emptied it over the desk, exclaiming with satisfaction as his fingers closed over the object he sought. He slipped the thing into his pocket. "Right. Let's go."

"But the effects. Shouldn't we return them, sir?"

"Later, man, later." Thanet almost pushed Bentley out of the office in his impatience to be gone. "If we don't hurry, we'll miss him."

Outside the building Bentley automatically turned towards the car park. Thanet grabbed his sleeve. "It'll be quicker to walk. Too much traffic."

Bentley said nothing, merely swung after Thanet who was setting off at a half-run in the direction of High Street. The pavements were filling up rapidly with people on their way home from work and already the traffic in the High Street was at a standstill.

By the time they reached Parrish's office it was almost half past five and Thanet was steeling himself for disappointment. If Parrish wasn't there . . .

But he was. Just. Thanet and Bentley reached him as he turned away from locking the door.

"Could we have a word, do you think, Mr Parrish?"

Parrish turned. "Oh, for God's sake! This is a bit much. I was just on my way home."

"Could we go back inside for a few minutes, sir?"

Parrish hesitated, frowning. "Won't tomorrow do?"

"I'm sorry. There's just a small point to clear up. It shouldn't take too long."

With an ill grace Parrish turned back to the door, set his elegant black executive briefcase down with a thump and fished the keys out of his pocket. He unlocked the door, pushed it open and stalked across the reception area to his own room. Thanet, who had been afraid that Parrish might have stayed in the outer office for the interview, followed him with satisfaction. Parrish's office suited his purpose marginally better.

Parrish put his briefcase on the desk, turned and, folding his arms, half-sat on the front edge of his desk facing them. "Well, Inspector?"

"Could we sit down, Mr Parrish?" Thanet asked. He wasn't going to let Parrish take charge of this session.

Parrish gestured towards two chairs and sat down behind his desk. As if to underline the proposed brevity of the meeting, however, he kept his coat on.

Thanet picked up one of the wooden armchairs which stood against the wall and set it down in front of the desk, facing Parrish squarely. Bentley sat down a little distance away and took out his notebook. Parrish opened his mouth to speak, but Thanet quickly took the initiative.

"It's simply a matter of checking certain facts, Mr Parrish."

"What facts?" Parrish made a show of pretending to relax, sat back in his chair with his hands thrust casually into his pockets. Thanet was sorry about the hands. They were always a give-away. He would be willing to bet that they were tightly clenched, knuckles white.

"Such facts as the precise time at which you left Mrs Penge on the evening Julie Holmes died."

The muscles around Parrish's jaw tightened. "At half past nine. I told you."

"Yes, you did, didn't you. The second time we interviewed you. The first time you told us you'd stayed at home all evening."

"I explained that. I was trying to protect the lady."

Thanet shrugged. "For whatever reason. The point is, that when someone has lied to us once we tend to be, how shall I put it, a little suspicious of him? And, of course, to check what he says very thoroughly. As we did with your story."

Parrish raised his eyebrows. "And?"

"And we discovered that you had lied to us again."

Parrish shrugged. "I don't know what you mean."

Despite his casual tone, however, his eyes had become wary.

"Oh, I'm sure you do," Thanet said. "Unfortunately for you, Mr Parrish, you happen to have been parking your car, on Tuesday evenings, in the space which custom allots to a certain local resident. And he's been getting rather angry about it. Now last Tuesday evening, your car was again in his parking space, and as he didn't know where to find you he kept a very close eye on it, hoping to catch you when you drove away. So close an eye, to be precise, that he went out every quarter of an hour. Your car was still parked in Jubilee Road at eight-forty-five, but when he came out just before nine he saw you driving it away. Needless to say, he was very angry to have missed you."

"Damned cheek," Parrish growled. "I've as much right to that parking space as he has. I'm a householder there, aren't I? I pay good rent for that flat."

"That, as you well know, is not the point. The point is, why did you tell us you didn't leave Mrs Penge until nine-thirty?"

"You're wrong," Parrish said calmly. "You've only his word against mine. And you yourself admit he's got a grudge against me. He must be laughing his head off, thinking of the jam he's got me into, lying about the time he saw me leave."

"Oh no, Mr Parrish. Not only his work." Thanet paused. "Mrs Penge confirms that you and she parted before nine-thirty. In fact, she says she left you at twenty-five to nine."

Parrish looked at Thanet in disbelief for a moment, his eyes narrowed into slits. Then, "The bitch," he said. "The lying bitch."

"I think not, sir. As you well know, Mrs Penge has everything to lose by making this statement."

The barb had gone home. "She won't get away with this!"

"Charming," said Thanet. "Can I believe my ears? A lady to protect, I believe you said?"

"No lady would behave like that. A lady would've stood by me."

"Stood by you in what?" Thanet said softly.

Parrish stared at him for a moment or two and then, astonishingly, began to laugh. "Oh no, Inspector, you're not going to catch me like that. OK, so I told a second lie. The very fact that you're here now proves that my reason for doing so was justified. When you came here the second time and told me that my car had been seen parked in the area, I could see that I had to come clean about Phyllis. So I did. But I made a mistake. A genuine mistake. I got the time wrong. Usually, you see, we do split up about nine-thirty, but that Tuesday I was feeling a bit under the weather. Things didn't go with their usual bounce, so I decided to call it a day earlier than usual. Then, when I thought back, after you'd gone, I realised that I'd made a mistake in the time. Now, Inspector, what would you have done? You told me yourself, a few minutes ago, that when someone has been caught out in a lie once, the next time you're even less inclined to believe him. So I thought it would be more sensible to ask Phyllis to stick to our usual time of nine-thirty, if she was questioned."

"You didn't think of ringing me up, to tell us of your 'mistakes'?"

"No thank you, Inspector. So far as I knew you were off my back, and I wanted it to stay that way."

"So what, exactly, did you do, after she had left that evening?" Please God, thought Thanet, he'll say he stayed in the flat for a little while, got straight into his car and drove away. To be caught out a third time in one interview might just rattle him.

Parrish narrowed his eyes, apparently in recollection. "Phyllis left at about twenty-five to nine. I tidied up, made sure that everything was secure and left a few minutes later—at about twenty to nine, I suppose. Then I went for a little stroll."

"In which direction?"

Parrish shrugged. "I really can't remember. Does it matter?"

"It might. Did you see anyone?"

Parrish shook his head. "Not a soul, so far as I can remember."

"At a quarter to nine on a fine May evening?" Thanet leant back casually in his chair, put his hands in his pockets.

Parrish lifted his shoulders, spread his hands. "It was getting dusk. No doubt there was the odd person about." He gave a pseudo-charming smile. "It'll be your job to find them, won't it, Inspector?"

It would if his ploy didn't work, Thanet thought grimly. He took his hands out of his pockets and stood up. "Right, Mr Parrish. I'm sorry to have delayed you." Thanet stooped. "There's something on the floor under your desk," he said. He straightened up, held out his hand.

Parrish stared at the enamelled mermaid, his face set. "That's not mine, it's Julie's."

"It belonged to Mrs Holmes?"

"Yes. Damned office cleaners. Can't trust them to do anything properly these days. It must have been lying there all this time."

"Yes," said Thanet heavily. "Almost a week, if it was hers. You're sure it didn't belong to one of the other girls?"

"Of course I'm sure," Parrish said testily. "She was my personal secretary, remember. She must have dropped it one day, without realising it. She used to take dictation sitting almost where you were, in that chair. I saw her wear it."

"When, Mr Parrish?" Thanet said softly. "When did you see her wear it?"

Parrish shrugged again. "Does it really matter, Inspector? It's hers, that's all I can tell you. It's a very distinctive thing, the sort of thing you don't forget easily, isn't it?"

"It certainly is," Thanet said. "Which is precisely why I picked it for my purpose."

"Your purpose?" Now, for the first time, Parrish looked rattled.

"Yes, I'm afraid, Mr Parrish, that there is no way in which you could have seen Mrs Holmes wear that brooch in this office. Her husband bought it for her on the way home from work the night she died, gave it to her after supper that evening. She was wearing it when she was killed. . . ."

Now at last Parrish understood the trap into which he had fallen and Thanet watched with satisfaction as the confident lines of the man's face began to blur, to disintegrate.

As Parrish dropped his head into his hands Thanet nodded to Bentley.

The words of the charge were music in his ears.

18

"So then what happened?" Lineham asked eagerly.

It was later the same evening and Lineham was sitting up in bed, looking absurdly young in blue and white striped pyjamas.

Thanet grimaced. "Oh, it was rather disgusting really. He broke down, grovelled. It hadn't been his fault, he hadn't intended to kill her and so on and so on. Says he went there on impulse. Since Julie appeared on the scene he'd been getting more and more tired of Phyllis Penge. Julie was a much more attractive proposition and the resistance she was putting up to his advances had merely served to whet his appetite. I think he genuinely believes himself irresistible and thought Julie's apparent rejection of him was a token resistance, put up for the sake of form. He was also convinced that if only he could get her alone, away from the office, he'd win her over. The trouble was that she refused all his invitations to lunch, drinks and so on and he was getting more and more desperate. The more she held off, the more he wanted her.

"The night she died he'd found Phyllis Penge less interesting than ever and he decided to cut their time together short. He says that when she'd gone and he'd tidied up he looked at his watch, found that it was only twenty to nine and remembered that Julie's husband always went to night school on Tuesdays. Personally I think he'd been building up to this for weeks. He was well aware that Julie lived only a few minutes away

191

from his little love nest. And in view of the night
school, Tuesday was the obvious day for him to try to
get her on her own. On the other hand he didn't want
to lose his present mistress until Julie showed signs of
being more forthcoming.

"Anyway, whether the decision was made on the
spur of the moment or not, he waited until he thought
Phyllis was safely out of the way, then set off briskly for
Julie's house. He arrived there just a minute or two
after Kendon had left—though he didn't know that, of
course. It seems highly likely that Parrish was the
person Kendon glimpsed turning into Gladstone Road
as he entered the wood to take the footpath to the
station. And Parrish remembers seeing a man just going
through the swing gate as he turned into the road.

"Anyway he claims that he put up his hand to
knock at the front door, but before he could do so Julie
flung it open and came at him with a knife, screaming
at him. Instinctively he put up his hands to defend
himself, grabbed for the hand with the knife, they
struggled and she was killed."

"But why attack Parrish?"

"My guess is that she thought he was Kendon. Just
think. The door of that house is half-glazed and Kendon
and Parrish are much the same height and build. Now
Kendon had been at the door just a minute or so
before, trying to get Julie to let him in. Through the
glass panel it might well have looked as though he'd
come back for one more try, and even when the door
was open Parrish would have had the light—which was
fading anyway—behind him. And I think that she was
in such a state by then that she was incapable of thinking
rationally. I doubt if she stopped to look at him, she just
launched at him."

"She'd reached the point of no return, so to speak."

"Breaking point, as Mrs Thorpe put it. Yes."

Lineham was silent for a while, thinking it over.
Eventually, "You said he *claims* that this was what
happened. Don't you believe him?"

"Oh come on, Mike. I believe the bit about Julie

coming at him with a knife and so on, yes, because it is
entirely consistent with everything else we know, but
the rest of it . . . No, he's just trying to save his skin.
Can you see him being so frightened by Julie's attack,
so little in control of the struggle that he has to kill her
to defend himself? Julie was small, slight. She wouldn't
have had a chance against someone his size."

"They do say that people who have gone over the
edge have an abnormal strength," Lineham offered
diffidently.

"Maybe, but not to that degree. I just can't believe
it. Anyway, it's not for us to decide, thank God. We can
leave that to the powers that be. But I have a feeling
that a good prosecuting counsel will make mincemeat of
the self-defence idea. No, I think it was deliberate all
right. Not premeditated, no, but I would guess that the
attack was the last straw for our Jeremy, as far as Julie
was concerned. I think he genuinely believes himself to
be God's gift to women and thought that Julie was just
playing hard-to-get. I expect he thought that if only he
had a little while alone with her she'd melt like snow in
summer. I bet he set off for her house as jaunty as a
peacock and what happens? She comes at him with a
knife, for God's sake! It must have been a shattering
blow to his ego, his vanity. He couldn't possibly have
known, of course, that she wasn't really seeing *him* at
all, or why she was in that state. So I would guess that
his instinctive reaction was anger. 'The little bitch.
Leading me up the garden path . . .' Something like
that. And of course, he had to act fast because there she
was, coming for him with a knife. He didn't have time
for second thoughts. So he turned her own knife against
her."

"Deliberately."

"Sure. Deliberately. Incidentally, Mike, something
occurred to me. You remember those two reports we
had, of a tall, dark man walking towards Gladstone
Road and how we thought the witnesses must have got
the times wrong?"

"Of course! You mean it wasn't one man but two.

First Kendon, passing Disraeli Terrace, then Parrish passing Shaftesbury Road—which explains why the sighting further away was five minutes later."

"Exactly."

There was silence for a few minutes while both men thought back over the case.

"Of course," Thanet said eventually, "we're still no nearer knowing who killed Annabel Dacre."

"You're going on with that?"

"No. Oh no, not likely. After all, there's no new evidence, is there? And Low did as thorough a job as you'd hope to find. No, I'm afraid Annabel's murderer is safe."

"But I thought you said you were pretty well convinced that it was Mrs Pocock who killed her?"

"I still am, yes. But being convinced is one thing. Proving it, as you well know, is another."

"It goes against the grain, though, to know that a murderer has gone free."

"Yes," Thanet agreed automatically. But he was thinking of the Pocock children and knew that they were getting on to dangerous ground. If there had been even the remotest chance of proving Edna Pocock's guilt he would, he knew, have had to take action. As it was, he didn't want to examine his own feelings too closely. If one started feeling sympathetic towards murderers there was no telling where one would end up. And there was something that had to be said. He braced himself. "So you see, Mike, you were right." The effort it had cost him to make the admission made his voice sound harsh, almost aggressive.

Lineham looked startled, as well he might. "What about?"

"About it being much more likely that Julie was killed because of what was happening in the present, rather than because of something that had happened in the distant past."

With the temperature Lineham was running Thanet wouldn't have thought a blush would be visible, but it was. It spread slowly up Lineham's neck, into cheeks and forehead.

"My goodness," said his mother, coming into the room with a cup of coffee for Thanet and a jug of lemonade neatly covered with a snowy white linen napkin for her son. "Just look at you!" She handed the coffee to Thanet, set the jug down on the bedside table and laid the back of her hand against Lineham's forehead.

"I'm all right, mother," he said irritably, with an embarrassed glance at Thanet.

She stood back, looked at him consideringly, her head tilted to one side. "I could have sworn . . . Here," she took the thermometer from the little glass of disinfectant on the table beside the bed, "just let me . . ."

Lineham waved it away. "Not now, mother, *please*. Later, when Inspector Thanet has gone."

Thanet could see why Lineham was finding it difficult to spread his wings.

Mrs Lineham's lips set in a disapproving line. "Very well, dear." She poured a glass of lemonade, thrust it into his hand. "Anyway, try to keep drinking now, won't you. It'll bring your temperature down quicker than anything."

Lineham took the glass without protest, waited until she had left the room, then set it down on the bedside table with a rebellious thump. He caught Thanet's eye.

"Women!" Thanet said, and was relieved to see Lineham grin. "Anyway," he went on, draining the last of his coffee, "I knew you'd want to hear how it all ended." He set the cup down, stood up. "Well, I suppose I'd better be getting home."

"Just a minute," Lineham said quickly.

Thanet sat down again.

"I wanted . . . I want to apologise."

Now it was Thanet's turn to look startled. "Whatever for?"

"For wasting your time, sir." Lineham hesitated, then went on, "If I hadn't slipped up over Mrs Penge, if I'd managed to get the truth out of her the first time,

then you wouldn't have wasted your time following up
the Dacre case."

Undeniably true, but Thanet somehow couldn't
bring himself to feel even slightly angry with Lineham.
Despite his own bruised pride, he suddenly realised he
didn't regret any of it. Dammit, he had *enjoyed* it. That
delving back into the past had rounded off his understanding of Julie, had satisfied his need to know.

"We all make mistakes," he said, "thank God. If
we didn't we'd be insufferable. I think we've both
learned something from this case. So let's leave it
there, shall we?" He stood up again.

"Yes sir. And sir . . . thank you."

Thanet raised his hand in a half-salute of farewell,
and left.

19

On a fine summer evening some three months later Thanet and Joan were strolling hand in hand towards the main car park in the centre of Sturrenden. It was Joan's birthday and Thanet had taken her out to dinner to mark the occasion. They were in a mellow mood, full of good food and wine, at peace with the world.

"Darling, look!" Joan was pointing across the road at a small art gallery which had recently opened. On an easel in the centre of the window, spot-lit from above, was a painting. "Surely that's *The Cricket Match*?"

They crossed the road to see.

"I thought so. Mr Holmes must have sold it," Joan said. "I'd have recognised it anywhere."

They studied the painting in silence. It was the first time that Thanet had had the opportunity to examine one of Annabel Dacre's paintings at leisure. And there was no doubt about it, he thought, she had been good. The painting drew the eye like a magnet, its jewel-like colours, distinctive style and crowded canvas a source of never-ending fascination.

"Did I tell you she put people she knew in them?" he murmured.

"Really?"

"Mmm. Mrs Manson told me. Look. I bet that's her, with her husband. He's wearing his dog-collar."

They leaned forward, pressing their noses against the glass of the shop window. The Reverend and Mrs Manson were holding cups of tea, standing near the long table which had been set up beneath one of the two huge oaks on the Green at Little Sutton, its white cloth gleaming in the shade. Yes, he would swear that that was Mrs Manson, Thanet thought, a younger, more vital version of the sick woman she had become. Extraordinary how, in such tiny figures, Annabel had managed to capture some essence of the person's individuality, so that they were immediately recognisable.

And there, he saw with a sense of shock, was Julie—no, not Julie of course, but her mother. Jennifer Parr, Julie's "spitting image" as Holmes had put it. The man beside her was presumably David Parr, Julie's father, whose tragic accident had triggered off the train of events which had culminated in Julie's death. If Jennifer had not left Julie with Annabel while she was in the hospital Julie would not have witnessed the murder which had had such a profound and far-reaching effect upon her. At Mrs Parr's feet, her yellow dress vivid against the green of the grass, caught in the act of picking a daisy, was a child of about eighteen months who could only be Julie herself.

He pointed her out to Joan, who grimaced. "Poor kid," she murmured. And then, "You mean they're all in this, all the people you've told me about?"

"More than likely, according to Mrs Manson. I wouldn't mind betting that that's Alice Giddy, for example."

Alice was walking across the Green towards the other spectators, supporting a woman who was clearly leaning heavily upon her—Alice's mother, Thanet supposed. Alice's glossy black hair was caught back in a chignon, accentuating the cat-like slant of the eyes, the high, prominent cheek-bones. Her strongly individual dress sense was even then apparent. She was wearing a sky-blue tube which narrowed to the hem, a complete contrast to the rather nondescript summer dresses of the other women.

Thanet looked for the Pococks, but found them less easy to identify. Was that Roger, at the wicket, and that Edna, bending over the pram of a neighbour's baby?

Peake and Plummer, of course, he had never met. He
straightened up with a sigh.

"Three hundred guineas," Joan said thoughtfully.
"Worth every penny, and a good investment, I should
think."

"No!" Thanet said vehemently. "I couldn't bear it.
Even if we had the money to spare, which we haven't, I
really could not bear to have that hanging on our living
room wall. D'you realise it was this painting which was
really responsible for sending me off on that wild goose
chase?"

"Poor darling. You still feel sore about it, don't
you?"

"Less now than I did." He grinned. "I don't know.
Perhaps it would be a good idea to buy it after all—
hang it up where I could see it every day as an Awful
Warning."

"Not on your life! Home is not the place for Awful
Warnings." Joan tugged at his arm and with one last
reluctant look at the painting, he yielded.

"There's no doubt that it is Holmes's painting, I
suppose?" he said as they walked on.

Joan shook her head. "None. I remember reading
somewhere that it was Annabel Dacre's policy never to
do more than one painting of the same subject."

"Poor devil. I wonder if he's still in Gladstone
road. If he has any sense he'll have moved by now.
Anyway, I'm glad to know he sold that picture."

"Why?"

Thanet shrugged. "Because it's rather macabre, I
suppose, to think of him having it hanging in his house
—unaware of its significance."

"You mean, he didn't know that all those people
were in it? Julie, her parents, Annabel's murderer . . . ?"

"He didn't strike me as being the type to be
interested in painting. The figures are so tiny, I doubt
that he ever studied *The Cricket Match* sufficiently
closely to have spotted Julie in her mother's likeness.
And he knew nothing of Annabel's murder. I did wonder whether to tell him, but I thought it would proba-

bly make him even more unhappy, give him a whole
new set of circumstances to brood over, just when he
was beginning to take up a normal life again. I don't
know. Perhaps I should have told him. Perhaps he had a
right to know. What do you think?"

A heavy lorry swung around the corner just as they
were about to cross the road and Thanet seized Joan's
elbow. They watched it go by and then he piloted her
across to the car park entrance.

"Mmm?" he said, making it clear that he was still
awaiting an answer.

"I don't know," she said. "I honestly don't think I
know enough about it to be able to judge. But, why
worry about it now? It's all past, done with. You did
what you thought right at the time, surely that's what
matters? What are you grinning at?"

Thanet's smile broadened. "Something Doc Mallard said to me once. 'Don't try taking over the Almighty's
job,' he said. 'He's much better at it than you could
ever be.'"

Joan's eyes sparkled with pleasure. "Typical," she
said. "But he's right, you know."

"He usually is," Thanet said. "Whereas I . . ."

"And so are you," she cut in. She gave him a
wicked little grin. "Well, most of the time, anyway."

They were still smiling when they reached the car.

ABOUT THE AUTHOR

DOROTHY SIMPSON, winner of the prestigious Silver Dagger Award, is the author of seven Luke Thanet mysteries, most recently ELEMENT OF DOUBT, LAST SEEN ALIVE, CLOSE HER EYES, and SUSPICIOUS DEATH. A contributor to *Ellery Queen's Mystery Magazine* and *Alfred Hitchcock's Mystery Magazine*, she lives in Kent, England.